THE UNPUBLISHED GUNN

James Gunn

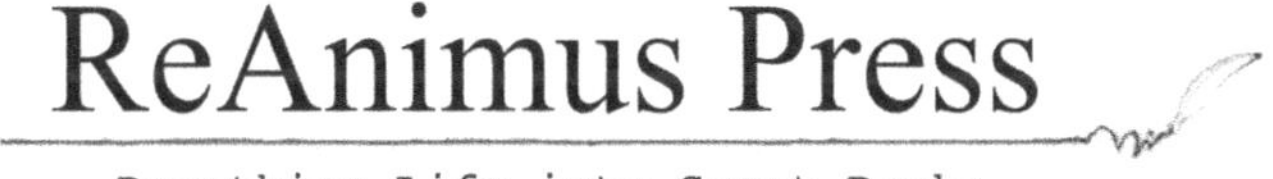

ReAnimus Press

Breathing Life into Great Books

ReAnimus Press
1100 Johnson Road #16-143
Golden, CO 80402
www.ReAnimus.com

Cover by Clay Hagebusch

ISBN-13: 9798554431937

First ReAnimus Press print edition: October, 2020

2010271106
10 9 8 7 6 5 4 3 2 1

Contents

PART I

INTRODUCTION

I started writing science fiction in 1948 at the relatively advanced age of twenty-four. In a field known for prodigies, I was a late bloomer. But I had excuses. I was relatively isolated in the Midwest. As a matter of fact, I did not meet another SF author, and scarcely another reader, until the World SF Convention of 1952, by which time I had been writing for four years and getting published for three. I also spent three years in the Navy during World War II, most of them in a series of schools and colleges as the Navy tried to figure out what to do with me. Then too, I had aspirations to be a journalist or a playwright or a poet, or the author of clever stories for the *New Yorker*.

Like most young SF readers I had tried to write at a more youthful age, starting a number of stories in imitation of my favorite author of the moment. At sixteen I even finished one and submitted it to *Astounding*.

What finally got me started as a writer was a couple of failures. In my senior year in college I wrote a play titled *Thy Kingdom Come* that became the first student play performed by the Speech and Drama Department, and on the strength of that I spent a couple of quarters in graduate study at Northwestern University before I decided that I wasn't learning anything about writing.

That isn't quite true. I did learn one thing at Northwestern. I took a fascinating course in radio writing. Out of it came an inspiration: I would return to Kansas City and write a series of radio plays based on Kansas City history. We put the idea into action in the spring of 1948, my wife and I, and even moved into a garret. But television was just over the horizon and no Kansas City radio station was interested.

I decided I had better devote my time to something I had a chance to sell. I wrote a 6,000-word story titled "Paradox," sent it off, and on the third try sold it to *Thrilling Wonder Stories* for $80. Looking back now, I can see that I started early in the history of the science-fiction magazines. *Amazing Stories* was only twenty-two years old, John W. Campbell, Jr., editor of *Astounding* and the founding father of the Golden Age, was only thirty-eight, and Isaac Asimov was twenty-eight. In 1948, however, I thought SF had been going on for nearly forever.

In many ways 1948 was a good year to begin. Not that I could made a living at it. I didn't write fast enough or sell enough at the time. I was writing short stories for the magazines, which were virtually the only market. Almost no novels were being published and few anthologies. Rates were higher than they had been, but still only two cents a word at most, and sometimes as little as a penny. In the next year I went through most of the $2,000 or so that I had saved while stationed on Truk Island, where one couldn't spend money except on nickel-a-can beer and nickel-a-pack cigarettes, and in the summer of 1949 I returned to graduate school on the GI Bill to earn a master's degree in English.

But the boom in magazines was beginning. *The Magazine of Fantasy and Science Fiction* started up late in 1949, and *Galaxy* began publication in 1950. Many other new magazines sprang up in the early 1950's some fifty of them over the next few years, and they all needed stories. I didn't sell anything to *Fantasy and Science Fiction* for many years, but I sold the early *Galaxy* half-a-dozen stories, including one of the first ten I wrote. Eventually I sold all but one of my first thirteen stories, most of them to older magazines such as *Thrilling Wonder Stories. Startling Stories. Amazing,* and even my long-time favorite *Astounding,* but I also sold a number of them to such new magazines as *Future, Science Fiction Quarterly*, and *Space*.

But this introduction is not about the stories I sold. Rather it is about the stories I didn't sell. It takes a bit of courage to present them here in this volume and its sequel, because they have about them the aura of failure. They weren't good enough. Even now, though, I'm not sure why. When I was writing them I couldn't tell the difference between the ones that sold and the ones that didn't. I wrote them all the same.

I don't make these stories available as object lessons in what not to do, although students of writing might analyze them, if they wish, for reasons why they were less successful than my others. Rather I think it would be good to give these stories a chance. They are only nine out of ninety-two, most of them among my earliest. It would feel good to have all my fiction out where people could see and judge it, not just those pieces that editors liked well enough to publish. These stories give me a feeling of something unfinished, of something I once loved and forgot for a while but now have rediscovered.

Here are four stories in this booklet, five in the next. Take them for what they are. If you find something to like about them, I will be pleased. If you find them flawed, perhaps you can learn from their mistakes.

I used a pseudonym, Edwin James, for my first eleven stories. It's hard to remember why. Maybe I wanted to save my real name for criticism, just as James Blish wrote his scholarly appraisals of the field under the name of William Atheling, Jr. But I began using my own name on my twelfth story, a novella titled "Breaking Point," and this piece, which began life as a play, may mark a dividing line. When I wrote "Breaking Point" I felt that I was writing with greater seriousness, with greater command of my craft, and with greater originality. With this long story my work began to be less inspired by my reading, more an exploration of my own experience, both external and internal.

The first of the stories included in this booklet is the fourth story I wrote, a novelette titled "Sane Asylum." I had ambitions for it. I submitted it to *Bluebook* and kept submitting it to a variety of magazines for quite a while. Fred Pohl, the agent that I acquired in 1951, submitted it to a number of other markets, including a non-SF magazine titled *Suspense*, but found no takers. This is the only story in the collection, incidentally, that I have changed in any way. I could find only the first draft, and I re-typed it with only such minimal revisions as I saw indicated in the manuscript or as I might have done in preparing the second and, what was for me at the time, final draft.

"Judgement Day" was my fourteenth story. It was written in 1951 while I was finishing up my master's degree.

"Broken Record" was my nineteenth story. I wrote it during the eighteen months in 1951-52 I worked as an editor for Western Printing & Lithographing Company in Racine, Wisconsin. Western published the Dell paperback books. I wrote only one story in Racine after that: "Tiger! Tiger!," which was purchased by *Planet Stories* but remained in inventory when the magazine folded; Chris Drumm published it as booklet in 1984. My experience as an editor in Racine came to a close in 1953 when I met Fred Pohl in Chicago at my first World SF Convention. Fred told me he had sold four of my stories, and on that shaky basis I quit my job and returned to full-time writing.

I made a trip to New York that fall to get acquainted with editors. Horace Gold, who had bought "The Misogynist," offered my a job as assistant editor of *Galaxy*. John Campbell, who had bought "Survival Policy," told me he considered it "space filler," but he talked to me for more than an hour. I also talked to Lester del Rey, who was editing *Space Science Fiction* and had bought "Breaking Point," and with Harry Harrison, who was editing *Rocket Stories* and had purchased "Killer." Evelyn Harrison, soon to become Evelyn del Rey, was working for the Dirk

Wylie Literary agency that Fred had taken over and was fascinated by "Breaking Point," but kept asking me to explain it.

On the train trip back to Kansas, I had time to think about the great figures of SF I had met, including Ted Sturgeon, and about the ideas I had picked up. One of them came out of my conversation with Campbell; the other came out of nowhere. When I was working on an autobiographical article a few years ago, I recalled that I sat down and wrote both of them in the next month, sold them both for a total of more that $1,000, and thought my future as a full-time writer was secure. But when I looked up the records I discovered that my memory was faulty. I wrote the first one immediately, it is true. Fred sold "The Saddest Man in the World" to *Argosy*, where it was published as "The Man Who Owned Tomorrow." Two dark stories intervened, story number twenty-two, "The Black Marble," and number twenty-three, "The Whip," neither of which ever sold, perhaps because they were too depressing. Then I wrote the other one, the joyful short novel "Happy Is the Bride," which *Galaxy* published as "Wherever You May Be," after Campbell expressed disinterest in the idea.

That's where this introduction should stop, between "The Black Marble," which concludes this booklet and "The Whip," which begins the second one, and right at the start of my second period of full-time freelance writing. We were still living in Chanute, Kansas, but we would be moving back to Kansas City early in 1953, where I would get a contract for my first novel.

James Gunn
Lawrence, Kansas

[Continued in the Introduction to Part II. Note the two 'Drumm" booklets have been consolidated as the two parts of this one book. —The Publisher]

SANE ASYLUM

Craig Randall slowly opened the door and stared, blinking, into the hall.

Three white-coated men stood quietly looking at him.

Craig woke slowly and unpleasantly. His legs moved sluggishly in half-sleep, and his tongue rolled thickly around a fuzzy and bitter mouth. He was still dreaming, and there was a ringing in his ears. It was insistent. It was ringing for him. There was no escape. He raced madly around the dull, gray walls of his mind. No opening anywhere—no window, no door. He had to face it—alone.

"Aline!" he called, and the name echoed around and around in dizzying, inexorable circles.

Craig woke up. The door bell was ringing. How long had it been ringing, he wondered, as he pulled himself erect and propped up his reeling head. Whoever they were, they weren't giving up.

Craig put his legs over the edge of the bed and caught himself as he was about to topple over onto his face. He felt like a week's hangover. That was funny. As he remembered it he'd had just a couple of drinks last night with—with—Aline. Aline, of course. And now he felt terrible.

He slipped his feet into his bedroom slippers. Why didn't they stop ringing that bell? It cut into his nerves like a knife; he couldn't think. And something was knocking at the door of his consciousness, something he should remember. He shook his head to clear away the fog, but it wasn't any use. It only made him feel ill.

That infernal bell! How could a man think when that bell wouldn't stop ringing? There was something—. No. He couldn't remember. He struggled into his robe. Standing up he felt sicker. Why didn't they stop ringing! He was coming. But they didn't know that. He opened his mouth to call but closed it hastily.

Craig walked unsteadily across the deep-carpeted floor of his bedroom and living room, into the little hall. At the door he hesitated. Who could it be? Not Aline or any of their friends. They knew he didn't get up this early. Maybe the landlady, Mrs. Jepson. Maybe a telegram. Maybe his editor wanted to rush the last chapters of his novel....

There was only one way to stop the ringing.

Craig Randall slowly opened the door and stared, blinking, into the hall.

Three white-coated men stood quietly looking at him.

One of them, a flesh-colored hearing aid plugged into his ear, stepped forward.

"Mr. Craig Randall?" he asked politely.

Craig gazed blankly at the tall, muscular, competent-appearing spokesman of the group.

"Yes," he said, uncertainly, something nagging at his memory as he steadied himself against the wall.

The leader nodded to the other two in the hall and brushed past Craig into the room. As Craig turned to face him indignantly, he heard the door click behind him. He wheeled again to find the other two with their broad backs planted against the closed door to his apartment. Their calm, businesslike expressions did not change under his angry gaze.

Once more he turned, becoming angrier at each revolution.

"What are you doing forcing yourself into my rooms like this? What's your business?"

The one with the hearing aid gave his shoulders a small, apologetic shrug.

"I'm sorry, Mr. Randall. Believe me, we regret these measures more than you do. In fact, our instructions insist that we proceed as circumspectly as possible. Unfortunately, we can never be certain of our reception. You can appreciate that, I'm sure."

"What instructions? Who do you work for? What do you want with me?"

"Oh, I'd forgotten. You *don't* know, do you?" The other gave a little chuckle at his own stupidity.

"No," Craig said, unamused.

"We're from 'The Willows,'" the man with the hearing aid said confidentially.

"The Willows?" Craig repeated blankly.

"The Willows Mental Hospital," the other amplified.

Craig looked at him searchingly, turned, and inspected the faces of the two behind him. None of them smiled.

"It's a joke," he said, without conviction.

"No joke, Mr. Randall," the spokesman said.

Craig glanced from one to another of them nervously. Then, slowly, his face began to clear.

"I see. You've come for information about somebody. Well, I don't know anyone who's ready for you—unless it's Tony Adams, who sometimes sees pink frogs." He laughed, but the sound seemed forced and flat in the stillness. "Fishing for green minnows," he was about to add, as he usually did, but somehow he didn't feel like battling the grave watchfulness of the whitecoats.

"So, unless you tell me what you've come for—." His voice trailed away.

The leader of the group leaned toward him with the happily expectant look of a professor about to net a priceless butterfly.

"Why, of course, Mr. Randall," he said with a gentleness that made Craig's head reel.

"We've come for you."

When Randall regained consciousness he was almost dressed. Somehow the attendants had struggled his limp body into trousers and shirt and jacket. Socks had replaced his slippers and one of the two who had said nothing since entering his rooms was slipping his feet into shoes but had not yet laced them up.

"Ah, Mr. Randall is with us again," the leader said cheerfully, as Craig struggled into a sitting position.

"Get away from my feet, you baboon!" Craig shouted. The comparison was apt, but the attendant left his task and stood up unresentfully. Craig turned his smoldering gaze on the one with the hearing aid. "If I remember correctly, you said something about taking me to an insane asylum —."

"Please, Mr. Randall," the other interrupted. "We prefer to speak of it as a mental hospital."

"I wouldn't go with you no matter what you called it!"

"Mr. Randall!" The attendant was shocked. "Everything is ready. The papers are signed and witnessed; your quarters have been prepared for you. You can't back out now."

"Back out! I didn't even back into this thing! You just take your talkative little playmates and run along. I can get along without valet service."

"Now, Mr. Randall," the other said soothingly, "you signed the commitment papers yourself. Just come along quietly and everything will be all right."

Craig shook his head slowly. The events of the preceding night were foggy, but not that foggy.

"You're crazy. I never signed anything like that in my life."

The attendant shook his head sadly. "A typical delusion. As a matter of fact, I have the papers with me now."

He held out the papers, just beyond Craig's reach. Even at that distance the concluding scribble looked to Craig's straining eyes like his own signature. He made a wild, futile grab that closed on nothing.

"Now, now," the attendant chided, as if speaking to a small child, while he carefully folded the papers and replaced them in the pocket of his white coat.

"It's a crazy plot!" Craig raged, and then a fierce light blazed in his eyes. "But you slipped up when you said a few minutes ago that I didn't know about it."

"You were rather—high, shall we say, last night," the attendant said smoothly. "But it's all legal—all perfectly legal."

"I'd never forget anything like that. No matter how drunk I get I never forget anything important."

"Then what did you do last night?"

"Well—I—." Craig thought for one terrible, heartstopping moment that perhaps he *was* insane, but he thrust the thought away. "I had a few drinks with a friend and went to bed."

"And that's all?" the attendant asked softly.

"That's all!" Craig insisted with an iron jaw.

"Then, Mr. Randall," the spokesman said gently, "I shall have to tell you the real reason you do not remember—a reason you must already have begun to suspect. You are a victim of an unusual case of schizophrenia, in which one personality is insane and the other is sane, with an almost complete memory blockage between the two.

"And I'm afraid," he added sadly, "that you are not the sane Craig Randall."

"I won't go!" Craig snarled.

"You will either go with us quietly or we will put you in a strait jacket," the attendant said as if he were tired of debating.

Craig decided to go quietly. He was no Houdini. There wasn't much chance of his escaping from a strait jacket.

As he was led down the stairs, his shoes flopping dangerously about his feet, his thoughts whirled in his head. It was true—he couldn't remember clearly what had happened last night, but then he must have drunk much more than he remembered. Was it one or two—or a dozen? Craig would have liked to have inspected the liquor cabinet, but he had an idea his attendants wouldn't turn back now. Wait a minute! As he recalled there was only part of a bottle left. He had intended to get more but had forgotten. So he couldn't have had more that a few. Or had they sent out for more? The memory was too nebulous to cling to.

Well, there was last night then—unexplainable at present. But that was the only time. There were no more blanks in his memory—or were there? Craig's head ached with the effort to remember.

They were downstairs now, and Mrs. Jepson was looming up ahead of them, shaking her head sympathetically.

"Ah, poor Mr. Randall," she sighed. "So young, so handsome, so talented. Such a pity!"

"Yes, madam," the man with the hearing aid said politely.

"I won't say that it was unexpected, though," she continued sadly, her fat, sagging face drooping even more. "He was like two different persons. Sometimes so nice and gentle and mannerly; sometimes like a wild man—like last night."

Of course, Craig thought bitterly. Sometimes he had a drink too many. And—last night, again! What was it about last night?

"Such a pity!" Mrs. Jepson breathed.

On an impulse he spoke to his attendants.

"May I speak with my landlady for a moment—alone. I'd like to make a few last-minute arrangements."

"Of course," the leader said, surprisingly.

They backed off, covering the lanes of escape.

"Mrs. Jepson, I want you to do something for me," he began in a low, urgent voice.

"Sure, Mr. Randall," she said, retreating a little. "Anything."

"Well, try and remember this. I'm being taken to the Willows Mental Hospital. Got that? Willows Mental Hospital."

"Willows Mental Hospital," she repeated obediently.

"That's right. By three men who say I have signed commitment papers."

"By three men who say you have signed commitment papers."

Craig nodded and thought swiftly. No need to tell her more. It might alarm her to hear him protesting his sanity. He stepped closer. "Now, get in touch with Aline Meadows—you know her. Her number's in the phone book. Tell her what I've just told you."

Mrs. Jepson backed away a little more, her head nodding slowly. Then a wary look came into her eyes.

"Aline?" she said.

"Yes. Aline," he whispered urgently as his guards came up again and began to hasten him away.

"Don't forget!" he called back casually.

"I won't," she yelled after them. "But, Mr. Randall"—was there a nasty note of triumph in her voice?—"it won't do any good. She was there last night when you signed the papers!"

The cot in the ambulance was comfortable enough but not so comfortable that Craig enjoyed being strapped to it. The gag in his mouth, on the other hand, was neither comfortable nor enjoyable. As a matter of record, Craig had objected strenuously to both measures, objections which were speedily brushed aside by the two ex-wrestlers employed as attendants.

After Craig had subsided into muffled, querulous moans, the ride began, a casual, commonplace trip through the heart of the city at a moderate speed. Certainly nothing to attract attention.

Nothing to attract attention. Craig's heart gave a leap. What could he do to cause an investigation? It was a matter that could bear some thought.

While he thought about it, the other three engaged in spasmodic conversation. Craig listened intently for a while, hoping they might let fall some key to the plot, but the only significant observations were that someone was pulling the favorites at the track again and that the Yankees were a cinch for the pennant.

The talk veered briefly to foreign affairs, to some of the nurses at the hospital, and back to sports. After a bit Craig stopped listening.

For a moment his thoughts sifted through the events and revelations of the last hour. What was it he wanted to remember? The commitment papers? Maybe—but he didn't think so. It was something else. Something important. Was he really schizophrenic? Bosh! And Aline—had she been there? He wanted to talk to Aline. Maybe she could clear up a lot of things.

He pushed the thoughts away from him. Right now there were more important things. It was a warm, summer morning and the back window of the ambulance was open. If he could only make a noise or yell, somebody would hear. But he was gagged and strapped securely. All except his lower limbs.

He could thump the side of the ambulance, maybe, but who would notice in all the noise of traffic? Besides, his shoes hadn't been laced up; they might fall off. He thought that over carefully. They might indeed. He swung one foot experimentally. Yes, they probably would.

Craig sighted at the window, peering over the gag, then flopped his head back on the cot and glanced quickly around. Nobody seemed to notice. He loosened the shoe on his right foot with his toes and swung his foot back and forth casually. The conversation continued unabated. The ambulance had stopped at an intersection; it was starting across the street. It was in the middle. Now. Now!

The shoe described a beautiful arc as it swished through the window and into the street behind. The ambulance moved on. Ten feet. Twenty feet. Nothing. Craig's heart sank.

Suddenly a whistle sounded from behind and a yell from a loud, commanding voice. "Stop, there! You in the ambulance! Pull over!"

The ambulance swerved right and shivered to a stop.

The padding of large, heavy feet grew closer and stopped with the appearance in the rear window of a florid, angry face.

"Who's throwin' shoes from this thing?" demanded a hoarse voice.

Craig made inarticulate sounds.

"What's that?"

The attendant with the hearing aid appeared in the rear window. "I'm sorry, Officer. It must have slipped from the foot of our patient."

Craig groaned.

"Slipped, eh?" said the policeman. "Well, how did it get back in the street? Came whizzing past my ear like a bullet."

"It was just an accident, Officer. It won't happen again."

Craig groaned as loud as he could.

"What's the matter with that man?" the officer demanded. "Sounds like he's dyin'." He moved over to peer into the interior.

"There's nothing wrong with him—."

"There isn't! Then why are you takin' him to a hospital?"

"He isn't a regular hospital patient, officer—."

The policeman's eyes narrowed suspiciously. Craig groaned again.

"I can see that. You don't usually put gags in their mouths, do you?"

"Well, no, Officer, but—."

"Take it out! I wanta hear what the guy has to say."

"Very well, sir," the attendant said, motioning to his assistants.

The gag removed, Craig burst into passionate speech. "I'm being kidnapped, Officer. Get me out of here!"

The policeman looked around warily. "Kidnapped, is it?"

"Don't believe anything these men have to say! They're pretending to take me to an insane asylum, but I'm just as sane as you are."

"Insane asylum," the officer repeated slowly.

"I don't know what their game is, but they're trying to get rid of me, one way or another."

The attendant in charge, who had been listening patiently, broke in. "Most of what Mr. Randall has been telling you is true, Officer. All except the part that he is sane. Here are our papers."

He handed over a small bundle.

The policeman glanced at them suspiciously, keeping one eye on the ambulance and its occupants. Slowly his face cleared. Finally he gave a little chuckle and handed the papers back. "A looney, eh? Might have known."

"Officer!" Craig screamed. "It's all a trick, I tell you! They don't have any right to take me. I didn't sign it, I tell you — ."

"Say! Maybe you better put that gag back in his mouth. Sorry to have disturbed you people, but it was kinda funny having a shoe whistle past my ear like that."

"That's all right, Officer. No trouble."

The policeman turned to leave.

"We'll take the shoe, if you don't mind."

"Oh! Sure. Got no use for it. Wear elevens, myself. Wait till I get home and tell the wife about this. Imagine that! Kidnapped!"

The head attendant shook his head sadly at Craig as the car pulled away, and Craig sank once more into muffled glumness.

The Willows might have been a rambling country estate with a long, winding, rather dusty road leading through the guarded, massive gates in the spiked iron fence up to a colonially pillared white mansion. The great sweeps of green lawn had a manicured look, and the small groups of people who wandered idly about or engaged in tennis or croquet might have been guests at a sumptuous house party.

But that easy assumption was jarred by the sight of heavy iron bars at the windows and muscular white-clad men and women following discreetly behind each group of happy vacationers. The iron fence was ornamental, too, but inspired the horrid suspicion that it could be electrified. And, as the ambulance turned a corner, a glimpse around the edge of the colonial front of the house revealed gray stone wings extending far to the rear.

Craig took it all in, noting each strong point with dismay but filing it all for future reference. He was sitting up now, having been released from his bonds and gag once the outskirts of the city had been passed. This part of the country was deserted, except for a farmhouse here and there, and any disturbances would only have resulted in further bruises.

Craig had a feeling of relief as the ambulance pulled up in front of the wide steps leading to the huge front door. Once outside the city, the ride had been boringly silent, a silence that was sullen on Craig's part, matter-of-fact on the part of the attendants.

The man with the hearing aid left the ambulance first, then Craig. The ambulance pulled away with the rest and around a corner of the house to the back, leaving the two alone upon the steps.

Craig turned swiftly and started up the stairs, ignoring the quiet footsteps of the attendant behind him. As he reached the top of the stairs, a portly, distinguished-looking gentleman stepped through the front door and confronted him with a broad, genial smile.

"Welcome, sir," he said heartily. "Welcome to the Willows."

Craig stared at him blankly.

"And may I add that I hope your visit here is a pleasant one, a very pleasant one," he continued. He included the lawn in one expansive sweep of his arm. "We have so many guests, and they all seem to enjoy themselves so much."

He beamed down beatifically upon the idly chatting, laughing, playing groups. He turned his gaze once more upon Craig, this time a trifle apologetically. "I don't think I was told that you were coming. What is your name, sir? I try to remember the names of all our guests."

"Randall. Craig Randall."

"Ah, yes. And what do you do?"

"I'm a writer, but if you're in charge of this place I'd like to know —." The sight of the other's ecstatic face stopped Craig's protest.

"Oh, a writer! We haven't had a first-class writer here since Mr. Poe died." His voice grew confidential. "And you know, poor Edgar did have his morbid moments. Sometimes he wouldn't talk for days, just sit and stare at a wall." He grew cheerful again. "Oh, it's going to be such fun having a writer here again!"

Craig opened his mouth to speak, but his eyes fell upon the other's shirt front where several large diamonds, too large to be real, sparkled in the sun. Before he could recover himself, the other was moving past him down the steps.

"Enjoy yourself," he said as he passed. "And if there's anything you want that you don't see, just ask for it."

"Who was that?" Craig asked when the jovial man had passed.

"Oh, that," the attendant said, and smiled faintly. "That was Diamond Jim Brady."

Craig was escorted into a modestly sized office off the main hall. There an efficient young woman tried to take down information about him.

"Craig Randall," she said, typing it out on a card. "When were you born?"

"March 8, 1920, if it's any of your business," he said sullenly.

She nodded absently and continued typing. "Place?"

"St. Louis, Missouri."

"Height?"

"Five feet eleven."

"Weight?"

"One seventy-five."

She glanced at him. "Color of eyes—blue. Hair—light. Any identifying marks or scars?"

"My left hand is missing," he answered bitterly.

She looked up at him, startled. Then she smiled. "You're joking, I see."

"He has a scar on his right leg," said the man with the hearing aid.

The girl glanced at the papers lying on her desk. As she typed Craig could see her lips forming the word "schizophrenia." It made him angry.

"Occupation?" she asked.

"Sex maniac," he snapped.

"Writer," the attendant supplied.

"Next of kin?" she went on, unperturbed.

"Napoleon Bonaparte."

She pulled the card out with a competent gesture. "That's all."

Craig swallowed his anger. "Listen, Miss. I know this is hard to believe, but I don't belong here. I'm perfectly sane. I didn't sigh any commitment papers. All I know is, this morning three men came to my room and forced me to come with them. How does a man get out of here?"

She looked at him without blinking. "I'm sorry, sir. I'm just a secretary."

Craig was handed over, mumbling, to a white-starched intern. He noticed, without thought, the incongruity of the hearing aid in the young man's ear.

Dazedly he followed the intern through what seemed like miles of corridors, each separated by a door that opened mysteriously before them. Craig tried to keep track but soon became hopelessly lost, while the intern silently traced his inscrutable way through the labyrinth of insanity.

Craig pulled himself together and tried once more. "Listen," he said confidentially, and a little breathlessly, "what does a fellow do to get out of this place?"

The intern went on silently.

"I know it's supposed to be a symptom of insanity to protest that you're sane," Craig continued in what he hoped was a calm, matter-of-fact voice, "but what would happen if you really got a sane person in here?"

Maybe the fellow was really deaf. Craig spoke a little louder. "How do you convince somebody that you don't belong here?"

The intern didn't change expression.

"Listen!" Craig's voice broke as it went up in a screech. "I don't belong here. I want to get out."

The intern finally spoke. "I'm sorry, Mr. Randall. You'll have to go through the proper procedure. I'm not authorized to accept an application for discharge."

"Well," Craig said desperately, "what is the proper procedure?"

"First," said the intern, swinging open a door, "you'll have to take the sanity test."

Craig sat in a straight-backed chair opposite the two doctors at the big desk. He had assumed an air of confidence, but he was uneasily aware that his hands were trembling and sweaty and that a muscle near his eye was twitching. Craig pressed his hands tightly together to control them.

When one of the doctors spoke, Craig almost leaped out of his chair. "We want you to be perfectly at ease, Mr. Randall," the doctor said.

At ease! Craig thought.

"We'll ask you a few questions. You must try to answer them as truthfully as possible. We have had considerable experience with evasion, so that will do you no good, and will, in fact count against you. According to the information we have here, you committed yourself."

"No!" Craig croaked. He tried again. "No. I didn't!"

The doctors nodded slowly.

The second doctor spoke, with slightly less precision than the first. "We'll begin with a word-association test. Answer instantly any word that comes into your mind—hesitation will be noted."

Randall nodded. The first doctor began, the second noting the responses.

"Red." "Sunset."

"Blood." "Accident."

"Money." "Comfort."

"Power." "Work."

"Crime." "Punishment."

"Lust."

Craig hesitated. The doctor continued.

"Greed."

Craig hesitated again.

The test continued for several minutes. Occasionally Craig hesitated when he was given a word for which nothing came into his mind. And then the doctor said, "Aline." And Craig responded, "Love."

Then his temper flared. "How did Aline's name get into this? How did you know her name?"

The doctor waved his hand.

"That will be enough of that test. Now we will give you a few sample situations. You will explain how you would act in each one."

Craig subsided.

"A woman has been bumped slightly by a car while crossing the street. She was knocked down but not injured seriously. If you go to her assistance you are likely to be subpoenaed and called to testify when she sues the driver of the car for damages. Would you assist her or hurry on?"

"Help her up, of course," Craig answered without hesitation.

"You have a chance to sell a painting you appreciate very much for a large profit with which you can add greatly to your comfort."

"I would keep it."

"Both you and the girl you love are overturned in the middle of a large lake. You have no chance of saving her, but if you leave her you could probable swim to shore."

"I would stay with her and fight until the end," Craig said.

"There is no chance of saving her," the doctor warned.

"I would still try."

"That's all," the doctor said.

"That's all?" Craig said. "You mean I can go?"

The doctor pushed a buzzer on his desk. The intern appeared at the door.

"Take this man to Hall Five."

The intern began to lead Craig away. He followed for a moment, dazed. Then, with a yank, he broke free and came back to face the doctors.

"What do you mean, 'take this man to Hall Five.' I demand that I be released from this place. I'll have you all thrown into jail for false arrest, kidnapping, and anything else I can think of. You can't keep me here!"

The intern was tugging at his arm. Craig was close to screaming. "I'm sane, I tell you! I'm sane!"

The second doctor tilted his head up and smiled. For the first time Craig noticed that his eyes were redrimmed and bloodshot, and his head wobbled. He was drunk.

"Of course," he said, shaping his words with difficulty. "That's why you're here."

Craig woke up sweating and terror-stricken from the grip of a nightmare. Three brawny, white-coated men with faces like gorillas were chasing him through the sticky morass of the night. They would catch him and try to put him in a dark hole, but he would break away until they tripped him with cords from their hearing aids. And he would fight free again to go sobbing with desperate terror through the dreadful darkness.

Lying completely still, relaxed, with his eyelids tightly closed, Craig savored the knowledge that it had been only a dream. Slowly a vague uneasiness swept over him.

His eyes came open. They saw the monastic white walls and furnishings of a narrow cell instead of the modest comfort of his own bedroom. The door stood open and the room was suffused with a ghastly blue light coming from a hole in the wall covered with heavy glass and a wire grating.

Everything came back with terrible clarity — the kidnapping, the ambulance trip, the sanity test. He sank back on the bunk, overcome with the despair of his memories. There was something on his temple. Craig raised a trembling hand and felt a dried paste. Gradually his face tightened and became intent. His body regained its vigor. He swung himself upright and his legs over the side of the bunk. His chin descended into his hands and he stared unseeing at the blue light.

Think! he told himself. You've got to figure this thing out. Once you know what's going on, you'll know what to do. There must be some plan behind this thing. They don't just pick up strangers and throw them in the bughouse for nothing. No, he thought sardonically, they put them away because they're buggy.

That's out, he told himself. If you're crazy it doesn't make any difference what you think. But if you're not—ah, if you're not. Then you have to think clearly. You have to put all the little bits of things together, all the clues that have been left scattered around. It will make a picture, starting with:

Of course. That's why you're here.

Just a little time, just a little quiet, and everything would fall into place. He was sane. He had to start there. But somebody wanted him put away, wanted him kept away. Who? Who?

He hadn't any mortal enemies. Some rivals for Aline, to be sure, but none desperate enough or smart enough to try something like this. No, it was something bigger and more complicated than personal vengeance. No one would benefit from his being put away. There was no money other than what he would earn. His writing had all been fiction; he hadn't written anything or said anything to injure anyone or any group. But he might!

It all centered around what had happened the night before last. Everything had changed at that moment. What had he said or done? If he could only remember. He needed time and quiet, time and quiet....

The nurse told him he would go out in the lounge now.

"No thanks," he said. "I'll just sit in here. But I would like to have a cigarette and a light."

She was hard and beautiful. "You'll go out in the lounge now."

He got dressed and went out in the lounge, which seemed to be a sort of combination smoking room and library, with armchairs, leather couches, and card tables. A dozen patients, fully dressed, were seated. They were reading and smoking. Two white-coated young men with hearing aids hovered nearby to light cigarettes and perform small services. It was like the lounge of a good club.

Craig sank into a chair, had a cigarette lit for him, and tried to piece his thoughts together. Things kept eluding him. He had trouble concentrating. People tried to talk to him. His attention kept slipping to a tall fellow with a long, flowing white beard who looked the way the Apostles should have looked. He was talking quietly to another patient in the corner, but his kindly eyes, shaded by the bushy, white eyebrows, drifted their gaze about the room until they came to Randall. They stopped, startled. Craig thought they recognized him.

The bearded man got up quickly and started across the room toward Craig. Craig half rose to meet him.

"Let's all go out and get some fresh air and sunshine," said an attendant near the door.

That was that. An attendant started herding them out of the lounge, and a nurse linked an arm with Craig and led him to the door. Craig glanced over his shoulder, but the bearded gentleman was being led along as carefully as he.

He was going to talk to that man before the day was over, Craig promised himself.

Outside the sun was shining brightly and the grass was green. No one would suspect that these happy groups of smart-looking people were under guard—until someone made a break for the fence and was pulled down and taken inside. That disturbed the routine for a moment, but then the gaiety resumed. Underneath, however, lurked an ugly note of tension.

A little fat man sidled up to Craig once the nurse had left him.

"You're new here," he said.

"Yes."

"I knew it," the other said. "I saw them bring you in."

Craig waited.

"Are you on the side of law and order?" the fat man asked.

Craig nodded.

"I thought so. I told myself: he isn't like the others. There's something different about him."

Craig's interest rose.

"We've got to stick together, you know. As long as we do that, we've still got a chance."

"That's right," Craig said. "How many like us are there here?"

The little fat man shook his head. "Not very many. But what we lack in numbers we make up for in courage and determination. Someday we'll get a chance and bring this crew to justice."

"There's nothing I'd like better," Craig emphasized.

"What is the penalty for mutiny?" the fat man asked.

"Mutiny?"

"It doesn't matter. Someday this ship will land—."

"Ship!"

"You mean, you didn't know? They have it camouflaged very carefully, but surely you can't mistake the motion."

Before Craig's eyes the man was weaving to meet the angles of the sea.

"It was a foul day when they took over the ship. I was the captain, you know. They swarmed over me and—." The little man glanced carefully around as he saw one of the attendants approaching. "Sh-h-h!" he cautioned. "Here comes one of them now. They mustn't suspect."

He faded away, and Craig was left with his dismal thoughts.

It was almost an hour later before the white-bearded man approached. Craig had shrugged off all attempts to get him to join the games that were going on. He wanted to think, but there was no chance here. Too much was going on; he was interrupted too often. Craig wished passionately for peace and quiet.

"You're sane," the bearded man began.

After so many disappointments Craig tried not to hope.

"I knew that when I first looked at your eyes across the lounge," the man continued. "I knew you were one of us."

"That's what the little fat man said," Craig responded.

The bearded man's eyes crinkled up. "I'm not like him," he said, "although I don't blame you for thinking so. Many people here are sane except about one thing. But the sanity I speak of goes deeper than that. It's not the standard definition, as you may have noticed from the questions of the sanity test."

That was something—the sanity test. He would have to remember that. It was another clue, another piece of the picture.

"There are only a few of us left, of all that have been brought here, who have not been forced to retreat into unreality."

"You mean"—Craig's voice trembled in spite of his effort to remain calm—"you mean I really am sane?"

"Of course," said the bearded gentleman. "That's why you're here. You must never doubt your sanity. That's their purpose. That's their victory."

Of course. That's why you're here. Those phrases again.

"What's the meaning of it all?" Craig asked. "What are they trying to do?"

"It is a conspiracy of the insane against the truly sane. That much I can tell you. More than that you will have to discover for yourself. This much I know: it all hinges on why they brought you here. What did you say or do just before?"

"I-I can't remember," Craig admitted.

Into the old man's eyes came a strained, distant look. "That's the trouble. I never could remember either, never in all the time I've been here. What did I say? What did I do?"

Craig felt a wave of pity. "How long have you been here?" He looked into the old man's eyes and looked away hastily.

"Ten years," the old man said. "But others have been here longer."

"It's incredible that it could have gone on so long without someone finding out!" Craig said.

"That's why you have to remember. Try to remember. So much depends on it. Every day some vitally important person is taken to an asylum somewhere. That person is lost to the world, lost to the sane; those people who could reshape the world."

Craig looked again at the other's face. Had he seen it before, or did he only imagine it? "Who are you?" he asked softly.

"I?" the old man said, glancing around carefully. Out of the corner of his eye Craig saw the attendant with the hearing aid, the one who had come to his rooms for him, approaching. "I am God!"

Craig started. Was the old man mad, too? Or had they driven him mad? Or had he noticed the approach of the attendant and decided to deflect suspicion? Whatever it was, Craig felt a surge of anger. Inside a quiet, sensible voice was saying, "Go ahead! What can you lose? It's what you want anyway." He had been kicked around long enough. Now it was his turn.

The attendant would try to insinuate himself casually between the two of them, Craig knew. He waited until the fellow's genial face was just in the right position, then he swung from his hip.

The solid jolt to his arm and the sting of his knuckles was satisfying, but even more satisfying was the sight of the arc the attendant made flying backward through the air to land limply on the turf.

Two other attendants rushed toward him. They didn't time it quite right. One reached him a step ahead of the other. He went down, doubled up, clutching his stomach. The other Craig sidestepped as fancily as any bullfighter and sent flying into another pair of whitecoats with a good strong kick from behind. The three went down in a sprawling, confused heap.

They all were rushing at him now, from every corner of the grounds. Craig laughed as he danced around, dodging the grasping hands, to land a good blow here and a clever kick there. Mark up their faces, he thought. Give them something to remember.

On the outskirts of the melee Craig glimpsed something that raised his spirits enormously: the bearded gentleman was slyly tripping the assailants as they came running up so that more of them were on the ground than encircled Craig.

"Come on!" Craig called. "Come one and all. You're all welcome! Get your lumps and bruises here!"

They came — swarms of them. Finally, by sheer force of numbers, they carried Craig to the grass. As they brought him, panting, to his feet, he laughed into their battered, bleeding faces.

The first man he hit was just getting up. He moved forward and said only one word: "Solitary."

Craig kept his exultation to himself. Now he would have time to think, time to remember.

The room was padded but quiet. Craig settled himself on the cot that had no uncovered projections and glanced around the room that presented no opportunity for self-injury. But his mind was bent on construction, not the opposite.

For a moment his mind mused bitterly on the form of insanity of which he had been accused. If one personality were sane and one mad, which one wrote his books? It couldn't be the sane one, because he was supposed to be crazy now and he could remember everything he ever wrote. The insane one, then?

Sometimes I think there are two kinds of people in the world, Aline — the sane and the insane.

He grasped at the memory, clung to it desperately. There must be more — if he could only remember.

His subconscious had dredged up that fragment. He would try not to think about it, and maybe it would all come back.

What was the best way to attack the problem? There were so many facets, so many roads to follow. Maybe the chronological method would be the best. He would try to remember every-thing of importance, beginning with yesterday morning, and perhaps the events of the night before would come back to him.

He'd awakened sick and dizzy-and he hadn't had that much to drink. There was something he wanted to remember from the night before. Mrs. Jepson hated him; she knew about his sup-posed signing of the papers and said that Aline had been there when he signed them. The sanity test. He would have to go over that carefully.

What had been the key words in the word-association test? Red? What did they want him to answer? Blood? Remember that. Blood? What? Murder. Money? Power?

Greed?—Money? Power?

What did those answers add up to? A vicious personality, certainly. A lustful, greedy character. Almost—insane or one whose emotions would seem to him to border on insanity.

What of the sample situations? What clues did they offer to the character the doctors were seeking? Anyone who left a woman in the street would have no social conscience, no pity. Anyone who sold a painting he liked very much would either be exceedingly mercenary or have no appreciation of beauty. Anyone who left the girl he loved to drown in the middle of a lake could not know what love was really like.

What did it add up to? A vicious, lustful, greedy person, without social conscience or pity, mercenary, without apprecia-tion of beauty, without love or knowledge of it. A truly terrible person. Were there really such people? Craig hated to think so—and yet, hadn't that been what the doctors had been seek-ing?

The Question has been discussed for centuries in religious and psy-chic literature only under different terms: like the good and the evil, the saintly and the demonic. The sane, of course, would be prevented, by their own nature, from discovering the division, believing, as they do, in the fundamental goodness of mankind and expecting others to act as they do. The insane would not be thus handicapped: they would realize that a huge section of humanity could cheat, exploit, and rise by the vigor of their unscrupulous, unmitigated ambition. Perhaps they even have an organization for suppressing knowledge of the division, in fact (here he had laughed). I wouldn't be surprised if they should wipe me out tomorrow.

He was wrong there, of course. Murder was too obvious and too public. How much simpler and less obtrusive to take the suspicious away to an asylum—an asylum run by the mad for the sane—where they could slowly be driven crazy.

And then what? Oh, yes. *Then they had asked Mrs. Jepson to watch for the delivery boy bringing another bottle.* It had tasted funny when she had brought it to them—but just for a moment. Then there no more memories. Just a blank, hiding—anything.

Of course. That's why you're here.

They weren't perfect, then. They made slips. Lots of them. He had to wait for one and take advantage of it.

How did they work it? It didn't matter much. Was his apartment bugged? Did Mrs. Jepson listen, her fat ear quivering against an earphone? Oh, well. He would see that the world was rid of Mrs. Jepson. They would have to be ruthless, fight them with their own weapons.

They were so sure of themselves. But wait until he escaped! And he would. They would slip, and he would take advantage of it.

Craig lay on his covered cot, in his padded room, waiting for an opportunity.

The opportunity was long in coming. The only break in the long monotony of the hours came twice a day, when a small slot in the bottom of the padded door was pushed open and a small tray of unappetizing food was shoved through into the room. The next time the used tray was removed.

At the first interruption Craig lay sullenly on his cot, staring at the wall. Eventually, however, his hunger drove him to gnaw furiously at the food. After he was finished, he threw the smooth, unbreakable dishes at the wall and went back to his cot to fall into an uneasy slumber.

He was awakened in what should have been the morning, but might have been anything in his timeless cell, by a voice insistently calling his mane.

"Mr. Randall! Mr. Randall! Your dishes, please."

Craig opened his red-rimmed eyes and looked around the depressing room. The slot in the bottom of the door was open. Craig spat out a string of curses, the general tenor of the words being that they would wait a long time before he lifted his smallest finger to do anything for them.

"No dishes, no food," the voice said.

Craig discovered that he was ravenous. He lifted himself from the cot and moved slowly about the room, stooping and cursing as he went. When the dishes and tray were collected he threw them in front of the door and went slowly back to his bunk.

A small rakelike instrument pulled the dishes through the slot and pushed in a new tray.

"Thank you, Mr. Randall," the voice said sweetly and went away.

This wouldn't do, Craig thought desperately. He was getting nowhere and had no prospects for getting anywhere. He quieted himself as he attacked the food. They weren't making any slips; he would have to help them out a little.

The third time the little slot opened the dishes were on the tray and the tray was in its proper place. Craig laughed—a little wildly and hysterically—as the instrument reached in for them. The thing hesitated in its sweep and then continued its task. Craig's laugh was wilder as the new meal was pushed in and the slot closed.

That night he screamed. It was just a little scream to start, but it grew until it filled the small room to overflowing and bounced back and forth from the walls in swelling crescendo. For variety Craig tried a long, drawn-out howl. It turned out so well that he used it exclusively for almost an hour. He closed with a few yips and barks and a final, high-pitched tortured screech.

When the voice came again, Craig responded with maniacal laughter.

Craig screamed and yelled. He tried throwing the dishes at the slot and was rewarded by seeing one bounce crazily upward through the opening. Presently the slot was closed.

After what seemed like hours, a small barred window opened in the door.

"Mr. Randall—" a different voice said.

Craig bounced around the room on all fours, barking and snarling like a dog.

"If you don't act better, we won't give you any more food."

For answer Craig howled like a wolf. In the intervals between his vocal offerings he caught bits of a muffled conversation beyond the door.

"...Pretty quick..."

"...doctors..."

"...tests...?"

Craig snapped at the white-clothed legs of the men as the door opened and they stepped in. They pulled him upright, one on each side. The one on the right slapped him a couple of times, hard. Craig's head rolled slackly on his shoulders, his mouth open and dripping saliva. His eyes were partly rolled back.

"He's cracked, all right," said the big one, on the right.

"What do you know about it?" said the other.

"I've seen all kinds of 'em," said the first, not taking offense. "He's a loon, if I ever saw one."

They walked down the long hall, Craig slack between them, his feet dragging on the floor, toes pointed back. They carried him a long way, through many doors, and Craig could feel them wearying of their load.

"Let's rest a minute," one of them said. "This fellow's heavier than he looks."

"Yeah. We oughta make him walk."

Craig waited until they were faltering to a stop, uncertain how to handle him or which one should hold on to him. Still suspended from their hands, he swung his body swiftly and suddenly. His left knee, with all his force behind it, exploded in the solar plexus of the big attendant on the right. Anticipating the slackening of the hands there, he collapsed to one knee, spinning around, and brought his right hand up from the floor. The attendant who had been on his left had a look of stunned surprise when the first connected with his jaw and rocked him back against the wall to slide slowly to the floor.

Craig turned his attention to the other one, who was climbing painfully to his feet. This time he gave him his right knee, under the chin, and flopped him over on his back.

Raising the one against the wall to his feet, Craig dropped him again with a straight right. The hall was silent.

Craig glanced back at the other attendant. He was lying on his back, unconscious.

From the distance came the sound of footsteps, smart and brisk. Craig glanced around hastily. No time for careful study. Two door, one on each side. Craig picked the one on the left. To his relief it swung open, revealing one of the monastic cells he had first occupied, now, apparently, vacant.

Craig went to the big man first and dragged him into the room head first. He hustled back for the second attendant. The footsteps sounded just around the corner. Craig pulled frantically, desperately. As he closed the door and leaned his back against it, the footsteps passed by.

He listened as they faded in the distance and wiped the perspiration from his forehead. It wasn't much, but at least he was out of solitary and on his own. He went quickly to the big attendant and bound and gagged him tightly with the man's own belt and clothes. The other attendant was more Craig's size. He pulled off the white uniform and peeled off his own clothes, fastening the attendant with them.

When the exchange was complete, Craig stood in white and the other two lay in their underwear, bound and gagged, one in the bed and the other under it. Craig considered his appearance and then glanced at the bed. He snapped his fingers. He'd almost forgotten something—the hearing aid. None of the attendants seemed to be without them.

Were they all deaf, he wondered as he adjusted the small case on his body and started to insert the plug in his ear, or-? His question was answered before he could frame it.

"Attendant one or three," the plug said thinly as it came into contact with his ear, "report to Doctor Bradley."

Suddenly Craig was brought to attention.

"Attendant seven eight," the ear plug said, "bring Aline Meadows to Doctor Bradley's office."

Aline! Of course! Why hadn't he thought of it before? Naturally she would be here. It wouldn't help to shut him up if she were allowed her freedom and time to put together his kidnapping and his speculations of that fateful evening.

He had to rescue her as well. But where was she? Where in this maze of locked doors and baffling corridors could he find her? Oh, yes—Doctor Bradley's office—she was being taken there, wherever that was. There had been two calls for him already; he must be high up in the hierarchy. Then his office would likely be off the main hall. If he could only retrace his way there.

Craig left the room carefully, making sure that no one was in the corridor. He peeked around the corner. No one was in sight.

Which direction? Craig decided to go in the direction the footsteps had come. They had been brisk and determined as if the person were going to work, not coming from it.

All went well as Craig made his way along the corridor, until he saw in the distance a closed door. How was he going to get past a door, he pondered—one that opened silently and automatically at the approach of the one of the attendants? If it were controlled remotely, his chances of getting out were slim indeed, but if it were an electric eye or something similar located in an obscure or unlikely place....

But it swung open as he approached, triggered perhaps by something in the attendant's clothes or his hearing aid.

Craig almost broke into a run in his hurry to get to the main hall. The long corridors echoed to his rapid footsteps, but he only succeeded in getting himself completely confused. Finally he came to a panting halt close to another intersection of corridors. A wave of dizziness swept over him, and he leaned back against a wall. He rested there for a moment, trying to regain some sense of direction.

Left, he told himself. Left to the main hall. Right is back to the solitary cells. Or is it straight ahead to the main hall? Craig decided to chance a look in each direction from the middle of the intersection.

He found himself looking into a smoking lounge on the right-filled with people. A few turned to stare at him curiously. Panic swept over him and he almost broke into a run, but then he realized that these were patients and attendants—and to them he was an attendant. He nodded to them brightly and turned to glance down the left corridor. There, he decided, was his best chance. Twenty or thirty feet down the corridor it started to widen.

He walked in that direction, stiffening his back and making his step competent and determined. As he moved on, however, his gate slowly speeded.

"Attendant!" someone called out behind him.

Craig broke into a sprint, unable to control himself any longer. Presently he was able to dodge around a corner and paused there for a moment, panting, listening for signs of pursuit.

There was only silence. That relieved him for just a moment. Then he reflected. He had made his task even more impossible. Even if no one bothered following him, the unusual sight of a dignified attendant galloping down the corridor would have to be reported. Once reported it would be investigated. Once investigated he would be lost.

He would have to move fast, before an investigation could discover—if it had not already discovered—that Craig Randall was missing and presumable bent on escape. The smart thing, probably, would be to make his bid for freedom now, but he had never done the smart thing. He wouldn't leave without Aline.

From down the hall behind him came the patter of foot steps—several of them. Without glancing, Craig slipped around the corner again, hoping that he hadn't been seen. Then he realized he was trapped. He couldn't go back the way he had come, and he couldn't cross the intersection without being seen by the approaching party. He would have to stay where he was and pray he was not seen.

The steps were closer. Craig pressed himself flat against the wall. The party was almost to the intersection. There were two of them—Craig could pick out the footsteps. One of them was a heavy woman and the other a lighter one, perhaps younger. They were past the corner. Craig chanced a glance.

In that split second, Craig made his decision. He propelled himself forward and catapulted into the formidable, stocky matron, knocking her down and tearing her hearing aid from her ear.

"What, what, what!" the matron exploded.

The girl had opened her mouth in amazement. Craig gave her one desperate, pleading glance that silenced her. Then he bent over the matron, with profuse apologies, while his foot came down on the hearing aid and smashed it.

"I never heard of such a thing in all my life!" the matron said as she regained her feet and her breath. "You came out of that corridor like a cannon ball. Can't you watch where you're going? Clumsy fool!"

"I'm glad I found you," Craig began, talking quickly. "I have orders to receive the patient from you and take her to Doctor Bradley. You will return to your own ward."

"What?" the matron said dazedly. Then her belligerence returned. "I never heard such an order."

"I received it in person from Doctor Bradley. It was to be broadcast as soon a possible. I heard it a few moments ago."

"Well, I didn't," she said obstinately.

"Of course not," he said, pointing at the remains of her hearing aid.

She gathered the shattered remnants on the end of its wire into her hand and stared at it.

"You must have done this when you knocked me down," she said.

Craig's eyes lighted up.

"Ah, here it comes again. 'Attendant seven eight, release Aline Meadows to Attendant one oh three and return to duty.'"

The matron was bewildered.

"Well, I guess you're right. I'm seventy-eight, all right. But I still think there's something funny."

She turned to waddle back the way she had come. "But listen to this," she threw back over her shoulder, "they ain't gonna like it when I tell 'em you broke the ear thing. I'll bet they fix you plenty."

With that malicious jab, Craig and the patient were left alone.

"Craig!" she said, almost collapsing in his arms.

"Aline!" he said, holding her tightly. "I didn't think I'd ever find you."

A moment later Craig's mind returned to more pressing matters. "We have to get out of here," he said. "Any minute may be too late."

"The front door is the only way," she said. "There's no other door, and we'll never get out that way."

He smoothed the dark brown hair from her face. "We'll have to be bold. We'll walk right out the front door, just as if we have every right to."

Gradually Aline became calm enough to lead them toward the main hall. "What is it, Craig?" she whispered. "Why are we here?"

"I haven't time to explain everything now," Craig said. "But do you remember that night?"

"That night?" Aline looked puzzled.

"You know — the night before we were taken away."

Her face cleared. "Oh, you mean the night you signed the papers."

Craig stared at her as if she had sunk fangs into his hand. His brain began to spin. "But," he got out, "everything I said that night was right."

"But, Craig darling, you didn't say anything!"

A strangled cry broke from his throat.

"Oh, my darling," Aline said, "what have they done to you? Have they taken away your memory? And they were going to cure you! You were so happy when you got the news that they would take you in. What have they done?"

Craig wandered through the fog, lost, dazed, until, at last, the sun came and drove the fog away. They were outside and the sunshine was warm on Craig's upturned face. How they had passed through the halls and out the front door without detection, Craig couldn't remember. But now they were out and the fog was almost gone.

He mustn't think about anything but escape. Afterward there would be time to piece things together, but now they must escape. They must get past the guards, through the gate or over the fence. Not over the fence—Aline was with him; it would have to be the gate. The merry throngs were all around him, talking, joking, laughing, playing—the carefree, unstable throng. Unstable. Like cattle that could be stampeded by the sight of a tumbleweed or the howl of a wolf in the distance.

In a low voice so that only those close around him could hear, Craig began to speak. Gradually his voice grew in volume until he was the center of attention and all the patients were listening to him, trembling.

"Escape," he said. "Now is the time to escape. Make for the fence. If you all go at once they won't catch you. Escape. They'll kill you if you stay here. Outside is freedom. Make for the fence. Climb over and keep going. You'll be free. Escape. Freedom. Everybody at once. Make for the fence. Escape! Be free! They'll kill you if you stay here! Escape! Make for the fence!"

They turned, desperate, wild-eyed, crazed, looking this way and that. It had to be soon—Craig could see the guards coming toward him.

"Escape!" he yelled. *"Make for the fence!"*

They broke. In every direction they ran, screaming, maddened. The throng of happy vacationers was turned into an insane mob, breaking down all obstacles, brushing the guards from their paths, unstoppable.

Craig and Aline kept among them for a moment, until they were past the guards. Then, as the rest made for the fence, they angled toward the gate. The guards there were looking nervously toward the mad fighting on the lawn and around the fences.

"Go on," Craig yelled. "We'll look after the gate."

They didn't need a second invitation. They dashed off, plunging into the melee. Craig opened the gate. Could it be this easy? Aline stepped through; he followed. He closed it behind carefully.

"Easy, Aline, easy," he said. "We mustn't run. We have plenty of time. Once we're past that tree we'll be out of sight. Walk slowly. Don't look back."

All the time his blood was freezing in his veins and pounding hotly in his temples. It was torment to keep his pace to a walk. He wanted to run, madly, yelling, like the insane mob he had left behind, clawing at the fence.

After they passed the tree, they began to run. They ran until all they could see was the smallest bit of the top story of the asylum. Then they dropped to a walk.

"You're the one who's mistaken," Craig said when he had regained his breath. "I never signed any papers."

Did she look at him strangely? He brushed it aside.

"The world must know of this terrible conspiracy," he went on. "We must awaken the sane, lead them to their rightful place in the world."

"Yes, Craig," she said.

Why wasn't she angry the way he was? Why did she smile?

"I'm going to return to this place when I've told the world my story. Then we will see who is sane and who is mad."

"Yes, Craig," she said.

Why was she smiling. It wasn't anything to smile at. Why was she smiling?

In a top room of the asylum two pairs of eyes followed the lonely figures down the dusty road that led, eventually, to the city.

"This is your responsibility, Doctor Bradley."

"I realize that. It's the only way to effect a cure. Such stubborn cases as this need the shock of reality to return them to the normal state of mind."

"Suppose he should do some harm while he is out—I presume you will take the responsibility for that as well?"

"He will be closely watched. We will see to it that he harms nothing. Besides, the girl will help."

"You seem to have taken proper precautions. That is all the directors want to be assured of."

"He will tell the world his odd delusion, and they will laugh at him. He will be brought face to face with the folly of his attempts. Within a few days—a week at the most—he will be returned here for final treatment. He will find the world cruel, hard, unfeeling, deaf. If will be a torturing experience for such as he. I think I feel a little sorry for him."

"Doctor," came the icy comment, "are you sure you aren't....?"

"Sane?" the doctor snapped. "Of course not!" His gaze followed the tiny figures raising their small cloud of dust down the road that led, however far it went, wherever it branched, always back to the asylum.

"But even the mad can have moments of sanity."

Craig Randall slowly opened the door and stared, blinking, into the hall.

Three white-coated men stood quietly looking at him....

JUDGMENT DAY

The Earth turned slowly on its axis. The edge of sunlight crept across the land, as it had crept for uncounted eons. The sun beamed down with its customary neutrality upon the same unchanging scene it had illuminated for a number of revolutions of the planet.

The Earth was much the same as it had always been: approximately the same relative distribution of elements, approximately the same mass—the only things that had been removed were some very minor excrescences from the surface. The face of the Earth was bare; stone and soil and sea composed its features. The stone had always been sterile, but now nothing stirred in the soil, neither the blind worm making its aimless tunnels nor the stirring seed sending out its roots in search of water. The sea, the ancient mother of life, was dead; its surface was disturbed only by the wind, and below all was as still as if it had never moved.

The face of the Earth was bare; with blind, stony gaze it returned the stare of the universe. The breezes blew with neither blade nor leaf to slow it now, only the yet enduring mountains and here and there a heap of rubble. The rains came and went on and behind them sluiced the unresisting soil into the sea. Nothing had changed.

Yet, one thing was different. Beside a heap of rubble that was scattered by the ocean's edge, the morning sun glistened on a silver shape that pointed, bullet-like, toward the disappearing stars. The shape had an oval door, and in the shadow of the door stood a figure.

The figure was man-like—that much was discernible under the suit that covered it from head to toe. But how to describe the difference? There was beauty that was more than man-like and serenity and wisdom—yes, most of all, wisdom.

The sun's rays penetrated deeper into the doorway, revealing another figure behind the first. Without turning, the one in the door spoke—although it was not speech, nor yet telepathy, but something between the two which was more than either.

"Dead," the Philosopher said. "Quite dead."

"Too late," the Psychologist, behind, said softly. "We were too late."

"I wonder if we were not always too late," suggested the Philosopher.

"Only the most delicate of instruments picked up the first rays, and by the time they were analyzed and their origin traced..." The Psychologist paused. "The second came soon after the first—and then all the galaxy knew."

"That, too," said the Philosopher.

They turned back into the ship.

"No life at all," reported the Biologist from beside an instrument whose green line traced an unbroken course across a dial. "Even the depths of the sea."

"An accident?" asked the Archeologist.

"In a way," said the Biologist. "A chain reaction was initiated in the atmosphere, radioactive carbon was formed, life ceased."

"How?" asked the Archeologist.

"Only the cities show evidences of direct destruction," the Philosopher pointed out.

"Suicide," mused the Sociologist. "Why?"

"For that," said the Philosopher, "we must go back to origins."

"Life sprang up here, as everywhere," said the Biologist, "from a single living cell. Through a process of division, multiplication specialization, and organization, this cell forested the land and filled the sea with life—life that grew steadily more complex and highly organized. Sea creatures adapted themselves to the land and to the air. Past blind alleys of development, attempts at supremacy through invincible size and impregnable defense, through prolificity and solitary stealth, life made its way toward its ultimate goal—the rational being."

"The rational being," the Philosopher observed softly, "for whom life is a trust, for whom the universe is not too large nor his own soul too small."

"What a strange mixture was here, then," said the Sociologist, "where rationality brought only an increase in the possibility of destruction!"

"All through their history," said the Archeologist, "I find evidences of a civilization continually held back by perennial struggle for futile domination. Civilization built on the ashes of civilization.

"And now at an end," said the Psychologist. "The last civilization, the last ashes."

"The stars in their grasp," said the Philosopher, "and they chose the dust."

"Somewhere," the Psychologist said, "life failed on this planet. Rationality failed to subdue the blind, animal competitive spirit and formed an impossible mixture."

"Something," said the Sociologist, "which combined the worst features of both."

"Now," said the Psychologist, "the radioactivity has died away, the planet is once more ready for life, but the world is dead."

"Should we...?" The Biologist left is unfinished.

The Philosopher shook his head.

"It is not our duty to set aside the sentence that was passed upon this world. The planet is dead. Let it stay thus."

A clear note rang through the ship. The Biologist glanced at the dial beside him.

"The world, it appears, is not dead," he observed. "There is life not far from here."

He adjusted his dials and bent over a gauge.

"Life?" echoed the Philosopher.

"In the sea beside us — very close."

"We must see," said the Philosopher.

In a moment the ship was in the air; in another it was hovering over the sea on invisible lines of force.

"This is the spot," said the Biologist. "It must be small. The signal is weak."

"We must see," repeated the Philosopher.

The Biologist bent over another set of dials, set them, and pressed a button. In the specimen room a small volume of water appeared. The Philosopher bent his head over the eyepiece. He looked up.

"A single cell," he said.

"And that is all — in the entire world," said the Biologist. He paused a moment and finally smiled. "It begins again. The long climb, the great — the greatest — drama, the inextinguishable spark of life."

"How could that be?" asked the Psychologist. "So long? And only one cell?"

"We must have brought it," said the Sociologist. "As sterile as our ship is, one cell must have escaped through the air lock and fallen into the empty but hospitable sea."

"We have been turned, then," the Biologist said, "into the unwitting instrument of fate, nature's fruitful hand resowing the sterile places of the universe."

"Can we take the responsibility?" asked the Archeologist. "With what has happened before?"

"We are not wanton destroyers," said the Biologist. "We should not kill a world with all its teeming possibilities. We have agreed that there was much that was good in this world; how much more might there be in a new one, with a fresh start, a clean new planet to grow upon. We are the preservers of life."

The Philosopher spoke and all were silent.

"You are forgetting that it is not we who destroyed this world but its inhabitants. A dominant race, moreover, sets the stamp of its character upon a planet, just as a room partakes of the nature of its owner. This world has been soiled; no amount of purification by fire can wipe it clean. If life is an eternal circle, as we believe it to be, then there is no hope that life here can be greater than it was."

The Biologist was about to speak, but the Philosopher went on.

"If it is godlike to destroy, it is even more godlike to create. If we permit life here to begin again—create it by our presence—we assume a responsibility for all the evil that will come, for all the sorrow and the pain, for the long dying that is life—the creation of life is also the creation of death. We are not gods. Can any of us assume that responsibility?"

The Philosopher looked at the four others.

"We must make our decision as all of our decisions are made. By a meeting of minds. This button will release the specimen into the sea; this will sterilize the specimen room and everything in it."

Their eyes met. The Philosopher pressed the button.

Below, in the specimen room, the cell began to stretch itself, to elongate, and, in the process of partition, died.

BROKEN RECORD

Would you like to have six months? Free? Six months all your own? Of course you would. Anybody would, but especially you. You are unique; you are the artist. The world, with its mindless hatred, has kept you impotent while your agony for creation grows cancerous within you. You have talent, desire, but they are racks for fools without the indispensable ingredient — time. Time is the key to the world's prison, jealously guarded. Here is your key. Here is six months. Time to live, to rest, to grow, to work, to do. Six months — all your own....

You stop reading. You stare at the half-dark wall of your room, unseeing, contemplating a sick, excited feeling in your stomach like the brush of a butterfly's dusty wings. *Six months! Eternity, it is all the time in the world....* You wonder if every reader feels like this. Out of so many, maybe it's just you. Maybe....

The sick feeling grows. You look back at the page. You read the second paragraph.

You stop reading, You stare at the half-dark wall of your room, unseeing, contemplating....

Now you are caught. You are lost. You cannot stop. There's a house. It's not far. You've seen it. You remember it. It's an old house, a big house. The neighborhood has decayed, but the house is not part of it. The house stands alone, more inviting by its age, mellowed by good living and quiet thoughts, peaceful. You've passed it and seen its lights shining in the night, and it made you think of a private study lined with books and a log fire blazing in a fireplace on chilly evenings. You could work there, you've told yourself, there where time moves slowly and thoughts are long. There, if anywhere, you could do what you've always ached to do and never had the time. Time!

It isn't money you need. You scorn money. But time, priceless, can be bought; time is not money, money is time, and time is basic. Without time you are nothing. A gift of time? A gift of yourself.

You read the rest of the story, but it slips through your mind unresisted. It's very short, but it has no meaning for you because your mind is filled with speculation and hope and fear all mixed up together like bread dough, and rising in it like yeast is that sick excitement.

You finish and you toss the magazine aside and you get up and pace, and you see your coat tossed over a chair where you must have thrown it when you came in, although you can't remember where you have been, but it doesn't matter because suddenly you think, *Why not?* And you think, *What can I lose?* And you think, *If I am a fool who will know?*

You grab your coat and you leave, almost running. The night is dark and a little cool, but you don't put on your coat because you feel hot, almost feverish. It seems a long way, but it really isn't far. And you're there. The house is just across the street.

You stop, looking at the house, and you begin to cool off. Inside the house, lights are on. The study window casts a warm, golden image on the grass. The door is open, as if someone has rushed out into the night, but open, too, as if to invite you in. And the light streams from the door, as well, beckoning you closer, saying, *Come* in out of *the cold.* It *is* cold. You shiver.

You cross the street and stand just outside the rectangle of light that lies on the walk like another door. Now that you are here, a queer reluctance holds you back. The open door disturbs you. An uneasy memory stirs but will not come awake.

But you're here. You can't stand outside on the walk, shivering. You walk up the steps, slowly, pulled into the warmth and the light. Slowly, because something tries to hold you back. You walk hesitantly into the house. You stop just inside the door and wait for a moment. Nothing happens; everything is quiet. You reach behind you, blindly, and give the door a little push to swing it shut. Everything seems familiar, as if it had happened before. Happened before. It sings in your head like a refrain.

The door clicks shut.

Somewhere, distant in the house, there is another click, but near, too, as if the house and everything in it had clicked sympathetically. Like the click a needle makes when a crack in the record throws it back into the preceding groove.

You shrug it away. "Hello," you call, tentatively.

You expect no answer and you get none. The house feels empty. Intuitively you know that it is empty. Although you expected it, the reality disturbs you.

Something important, some part of you, seems to be slipping away. You brush your hand across your forehead.

You walk through the house, looking for something—someone. Slowly at first, then faster and faster until you are running, breathless with a nameless fear. A living room, comfortable, inviting. A dining room set for one, silver and crystal glistening in the light of the old-fashioned chandelier. A kitchen, clean, polished, stocked with an endless supply of food.

You don't stop to inspect these things. You know them. On the other side of the hall is a bathroom and then the study. The study is just as you imagined it; there is even a fire blazing in the fireplace. But you can't stop to enjoy it. There is no time.

You run up the long staircase. All the bedrooms are dark except the largest one. It has a big bed, freshly made, one corner of the coverlet turned back invitingly. It doesn't invite you. You run back down the stairs, back to the study. You stand there, panting, trembling.

The good living is here, of course, and the quiet thoughts and the peace. But it isn't your life, your thoughts, your peace. There is time here, but it isn't your time.

You have to think harder to remember things.

There is something on the desk. You walk to it, look down. It is a sheet of paper, typewritten. You read it.

I HATE YOU

Time is a circle. It is only necessary to shorten the radius. Here is your six months. Here is your six months. Here is your six months. Here is YOUR *six months....*

Your mind spins. The note is meaningless. Who can hate you?

Nobody hates you. You haven't done anything. The thought of hatred, nameless and motiveless, closes around you darkly, squeezing you in upon yourself, tearing at your insides.

Suddenly you don't like this house. It terrifies you. You run to the front door to get out. There is no door knob on the inside. Panting, you scrabble at the edge of the door for several minutes. It is futile. You stop. You look down at your fingers. The tips are bleeding.

You run back to the study. You try to open the windows but they are immovable. They are solid, one sheet of glass set in a frame; they were not meant to open. Wildly, you look around. You grab the poker from the fireplace. You swing the poker back and bring it crashing down against the glass. The poker rebounds as if the glass were a wall of rubber. You stand still for a moment, your breath sobbing in your throat, while your mind dashes madly in all directions. You need time to think. Time!

You run back to the front door. You are a little calmer now. It is because you can't concentrate, even on your fear. Thoughts keep slipping away. You notice blood on the edge of the door, but you ignore it. Except for a small window in the middle, the door is a solid slab of wood. The hinges! They are solid and heavy, but they have screws. Hopeless, you know that whatever you use as a screwdriver will slip from the screws as if they were made of glass.

Glass! You look down at the poker in your hand; you had forgotten that you still held it. You raise it again, bringing it down hard against the little window. The poker bounces back. You are trapped. You have exchanged one prison for another.

You feel a sudden sickness, not the sickness of excitement this time, but another kind. You peer out the little window in the door and notice that it is growing light outside. You refuse to believe that it can be dawn; you haven't' been in the house that long. In the combined light of the rising sun and the hall light streaming past your head, you notice something on the mailbox, waiting for the mailman to take it away. It is an envelope. You crane your neck, trying to read the address, but all you can make out is:

E-D-I-T-O-

And then you know how thoroughly you are trapped and why you are sick and why things feel familiar and that you can never escape, never in eternity, never....

Time is a circle, it is only necessary to shorten the radius. Your own private eternity. It is a trap, irresistibly baited by someone who hates you. *Why oh why oh why?* Somewhere, six months ahead, the snake will swallow his tail. For you know, dimly, and it is the last thing your fading memory remembers as you turn bewilderedly away from the door, what is in the envelope waiting on the porch. It is a story that begins (how does it go?)....

Would you like to have six months? Free? Six months all your own?

THE BLACK MARBLE

Dean studied the setup, frowning. The frown fell into place naturally, deepening the lines and creases on his tanned forehead and between his blue eyes. He looked middle-aged. He was not quite thirty.

The object of his frown was partly bolted to the table in front of him and partly strung haphazardly along its top. The bolted part looked like a miniature arched trellis, only instead of rose vines there were wires, hundreds of them, winding around and around and flat across the table. Or perhaps it looked more like a cathedral window, ten inches high, staring at nothing. Well, not exactly nothing. It stared at another arched window, equally blank, at the other end of the table. Attached to each one was an apparently miscellaneous assortment of tubes, wires, rheostats, condensers, power lines....

Tentatively, uncertainly, Dean reached into the maze and adjusted the setting of a rheostat. He stepped back and shrugged.

"Okay, Phil," he sighed, "let's try it again."

The dark-haired young man at the other end of the table looked over the collection of objects in front of him: a six-penny nail, an aluminum car key, a shapeless lump of putty, a plastic glass, a tennis ball....

Phil picked up the tennis ball and bounced it on the floor. Catching it, he placed it carefully on the table, in the precise middle of the window.

"If this doesn't work," he said, "we can always roll it."

He turned to a wall panel of switches and dials. He closed a large copper switch. Gauge needles began a slow climb. Tubes glowed on the table. Recorders scratched.

Dean stared at the window in front of him. Five seconds. Ten seconds. He rubbed his eyes. It was still there. Something dim, ghostly, and round was in the window. Something about the size of a tennis ball. Fifteen seconds. It grew no more distinct.

"Still there?" Dean asked, not looking up, as if afraid that the ghost might disappear if he took his eyes away for an instant.

"Hasn't quivered."

Dean put his hand out to his side and fumbled with an assortment of tools on the table. By feel, he picked out a pair of plastic tongs. Carefully he extended them, open, toward the shadow in the window. The tips of the tongs neared it....

A tube went dark. A circuit breaker slammed open. Dean's hand jerked.

The ghost in the little window had disappeared.

Dean threw the tongs against the concrete floor and cursed.

"Well, I'll be damned!" Phil said wonderingly. As Dean looked up Phil caught something in his hand. He held it up. It was the tennis ball. "It rolled out of the sender and almost off the table," Phil said.

"No joke?" Dean walked quickly to the other end of the table.

"No joke. You must have given it a push. Don't ask me how."

Dean took the tennis ball and stared at it for a moment. A muscle twitched in his jaw. "Oh, hell!" he said wearily, putting it down. "It's just another meaningless phenomenon. We'll never be able to do it again. Teleportation is a physical impossibility today. Working like this, without theory, it will take us a hundred years just to exhaust the leads we can see now. Maybe in a hundred years they'll have the time and the money and the brains and the equipment to do it. But, more likely, by then the Simpson Effect and the whole idea will be forgotten."

"Not to mention that our budget comes up for renewal in three months."

"Let's wrap it up for the night," Dean sighed. He jotted down the rheostat setting in his notebook.

Phil opened the panel switch. The tubes went dark. He turned back. "You're working too hard, Dean, and worrying too much. You ought to get out more, see people. Mary would want you to."

"I can't." Dean looked up, his face drawn and tired.

"Have you seen the X rays?"

Dean nodded. "It's a tumor. Just a little thing, Phil, about the size of a marble. But the doctors say she can't live more than a few months without an operation, and they're afraid to operate. It's too close to the medulla oblongata, maybe even touching it."

"Can't they do anything?"

"They're trying X rays." Dean's face hardened and he blinked rapidly. When he spoke again his voice was dull and lifeless. "Funny thing, the medulla oblongata. It doesn't feel; it doesn't think. It's an independent little robot that jerks your hand away from an unexpected sensation and keeps you breathing and your blood circulating and your food digesting, even if you don't want it to. Damage it and you die."

Phil started to say something and stopped himself.

After a moment Dean turned to stare moodily over the table, at the two empty windows. "It should work, Phil. I've got a hunch it's just a matter of tuning. The sender and the receiver have to be identical."

"Same number of windings," Phil said. "Same distance apart. Same number of tubes. Everything."

"Similar but not identical. Even if we duplicated everything down to a ten-thousandth of an inch, there would still be molecular differences."

Phil stared at Dean. "You mean we might as well give up?"

"I don't know," Dean said. "Maybe that's the wrong way to think about it. Maybe it's a matter of sympathy, like a fragile glass and a violin string. If we could just drag one thing through," he brooded, "I think they would tune themselves. Like getting wires through a conduit. You tie a light line to a ferret and send it through first. Then the only limit is the size and shape of the conduit."

"That reminds me of an old recipe. 'First catch a ferret....'"

"Exactly. Everything we use to pull with, shorts something. It must be something immaterial, some force...."

"You sound like Dr. Kleinman," Phil said.

"Kleinman?"

"The Psychology prof who has been investigating psychic phenomena. Didn't you see the invitation on the bulletin board?"

Dean shook his head.

"He's conducting some kind of demonstration in his home tonight. Invited all the physical science staff. Says he will supply definite proof of psychic powers. I don't know what, exactly. Telepathy. Telekinesis. Spirit voices. Why don't you come with me? Maybe you'll find just what you're looking for." Phil laughed.

"Sure," Dean said. "Just the thing." His voice was harsh and unhappy.

They walked to the door. Dean flicked off the light switch and turned back for a last look. The little windows were dark pools of shadow.

"Even if such an ability existed," Dean said, "there would be one big difficulty. The person who had it"—he paused and waved a hand at the cluttered table top—"what would he want with all this?"

Kleinman's house was a large stone mansion close to the university. The upper floor was dark, the bottom windows brilliantly lighted. Against the clouded night sky, the house seemed peculiarly foreshortened and amorphous, as it was half in this world and half in another and had not decided which to belong to.

A cold wind chilled them as Dean stopped at the top of the long steps. His hands were stuck deep in his pockets; his eyes were fixed on the sidewalk. "I think I'd better go to the hospital," he said.

Phil took his arm and led him to the front door. "Nonsense. You said yourself that you couldn't see Mary tonight, and the hospital knows where to reach you in an emergency." Phil pushed the doorbell.

Kleinman himself opened the door for them and peered at them, his long, gray hair ruffled comically around an open oval of pink scalp. His eyes were crinkled with laughter, and he greeted them happily and ushered them into a large living room.

"Whisky, ice, and whatever you want on the buffet there," he said as he took their coats. "Mix your own."

There were already seven or eight people in the room. Dean knew them all: Frederickson, head of the chemistry department, long-faced, serious; Burris, physics, short, egg-bald, nominal supervisor of Dean's project....

Dean hadn't expected to see them here. He nodded, sheepishly.

"Celebrating already?" Phil was saying to Kleinman.

"Oh, yes, yes," Kleinman said jovially. "No doubt about it this time. I have the proof. No doubt at all." He chuckled and bustled away.

Phil stared after him, shaking his head. "He'd be the last guy you'd think would go off his rocker over something like this."

Dean smiled wryly. "That's probably what they're saying about us."

Burris motioned for them to join him. Dean walked over to where Burris and Frederickson were standing with glasses in their hands, but Phil disappeared.

"Come to see the fun, Simpson?" Burris said, laughing.

"The fun?" Dean repeated.

"Old Kleinman make a fool of himself again. We tried to stop him, you know. Told him the entire project was invalid on the face of it. No measurable force, no measurable result. Works all the time or not at all. Told him. Hundreds of times. Eh, Fred?"

"An absurd waste of time and money," Frederickson said. "But I don't care if he makes a fool of himself in private as long as he doesn't cast ridicule on the university and doubt on more worthwhile projects. Luckily, the faculty senate passed a ruling that all research must be reviewed by an appropriate committee before being released to the public. That's the only reason I'm here."

Phil appeared and folded Dean's hand around a cold glass.

"How's your project coming, Simpson?" Burris asked solicitously.

Dean shrugged his shoulders. "Slow."

"Of course." Burris smiled pleasantly. "You will remember that I had doubts of its feasibility from the start. You will forgive me for thinking that it's allied somehow with this sort of thing, isn't it?" He waved a hand at the room. "Something out of nothing? Say, maybe you're here to pick up a few pointers, eh, Simpson?" He chuckled.

Dean flushed. "Maybe," he said, and turned away. He started walking toward the other end of the room, where a door led into the hall.

"Oh, Simpson," Burris called after him, "how's your wife?"

Dean pretended that he had not heard. "Pitiful case," Burris said loudly. "Brain tumor, you know. Inoperable. Tragic thing. Completely unstrung him."

Dean walked blindly into the hall and leaned his forehead against the cool wood of the paneling. A hand dropped on his shoulder.

"Take it easy, fellow," Phil said. "Drink up."

Dean stared at the ice cubes floating in his drink. "The drunken old bastard," he muttered.

"He's not so drunk."

"What do you mean?"

"That's what I've been trying to tell you," Phil said. "Unless we have something to show when our budget comes up for consideration, Burris is going to sabotage the project. He's been sowing a few seeds here and there, casually, about impracticality and incompetence. We eat up a lot of money, you know. He'd like nothing better than for you to go berserk and give him grounds for dismissal. Don't give him the chance."

Dean shook his head. "He's never been this bad before. There's something wrong with him tonight."

Phil smiled sourly. "You haven't been to as many of these faculty inquisitions as I have. That's typical knifework. Although it seems to me that everyone's a little more bloodthirsty than usual. I expect to see someone's throat cut before the evenings over."

"I hope it's Burris's," Dean said savagely. "Go on back, Phil. Don't let him follow me out here. I might be tempted to do it myself."

Phil patted him on the shoulder and left. Dean took a long pull at his drink and walked a little farther along the hall where it was darker and cooler. He felt feverish. He wondered if he was coming down with a cold. He leaned against a double door.

Something clicked. A line of light sprang through a crack between the doors.

"Ah, here you are, Willy," Kleinman said on the other side. "I've been looking for you. What were you doing sitting here in the dark?"

Silently Dean started to move away. Then he saw Burris, at the other end of the hall, peering into the darkness. An eavesdropper or a victim?

Dean shivered and retreated.

"I ain't gonna do it," said a high-pitched voice, like a child's. It sounded sullen and defiant.

"Of course you are," Kleinman said cheerfully. "This is what we've been working toward all there months."

"I don't care," said the other voice. "I ain't gonna do it."

"Now, now," Kleinman said placatingly. "You've done it dozens of times. This is no different from any of the others."

"It is so. They's others. They don't want me to do it. I can feel 'em."

"Of course they don't. They'd hate it. That's all the more reason to prove that they're the fools. They'll be the ones to stand there with their jaws dropping. We'll show them, Willy. We'll show the whole world."

"No we won't," Willy said stubbornly. "I ain't gonna do it." His voice was shrill with determination.

"Yes you will!" Kleinman was forceful and dominant and something else which was a little ugly. "I've taken you into my home and fed you. The clothes on your back are mine. Now you'll carry through with this demonstration or you'll go back into the streets where you came from."

"I don't care," Willy said sullenly.

Kleinman's voice changed. He began to plead. "I'll get you that bicycle you want."

Willy laughed, triumphantly. "Already got a bicycle."

"Oh, you have," Kleinman said slowly. "How? Without money? Then I'll not only throw you out in the street, I'll turn you over to the police for stealing from me."

"I didn't!" Now Willy sounded scared.

"Then you stole the bicycle!" It was Kleinman's turn to be triumphant. "You wouldn't like what the police would do to you, Willy—"

Willy muttered something Dean didn't understand.

"They'll beat you with rubber hose," Kleinman went on. "You know why they use rubber hose, Willy. So it won't leave any marks—"

"All right, all right," Willy screamed. His voice was filled with hate. "I said I'd do it."

"That's fine, Willy," Kleinman said soothingly. "That's a good boy. We understand each other...."

Dean looked up and saw that Burris was gone. He walked away from the double door feeling sick inside.

As soon as Dean stepped into the living room, Burris cornered him. He was contrite.

"Dean," he said, "if I said something I shouldn't have said, I'm sorry." He reached up to put an arm around Dean's shoulder. "You know I have the highest respect for you and your work. But all of us investigate blind alleys sometime in our lives. We all notice fascinating phenomena that lead us nowhere. It is an indication of our stature when we can recognize the truth of the situation and get back to the through street of modern science and research. I'm sure, Dean, that you have that stature."

Dean stared at Burris stonily, resisting an impulse to shrug the physicist's arm off his shoulder.

"These witches' sabbaths always upset me," Burris muttered. "You must forgive me, Dean. I'm not myself. We're still fighting the age-old battle against superstition. We're a fortress of enlightenment surrounded by darkness. We must keep our ranks closed up. What kind of natural force is it that works according to whim? What kind of world would that be?"

Dean shrugged and Burris's arm fell away. Before he could say anything more, Kleinman was standing in the doorway, beaming.

"Now, gentlemen," he said, "if you are ready, we will proceed with the demonstration."

Dean seized the opportunity to escape from Burris and join Phil. They brought up the rear of the small procession which trooped into a paneled library, rich with dark highlights and softly glowing leather bindings. On the floor, in a corner, was a telephone. In the center of the room was a sturdy pedestal table covered with black velvet. The only other piece of furniture was a folding chair close to the table.

Without directions, they formed a circle around the table and stood, shifting uneasily from foot to foot. In spite of his precautions, Dean found Burris standing on his right. Dean glanced around the room. The only calm person in the room seemed to be Kleinman. In this room he seemed taller and more forceful.

"We are here for a demonstration of the physical reality of psychic power," Kleinman began, "so I will not take up your time with more than a brief historical sketch.

"As you all know, a belief in psychic powers was the philosophic basis for pre-modern science. The emergence of industrialism and physical research pushed psychic and other less tangible phenomena outside the realm of the acceptable.

"Science," Kleinman continued, glancing around slyly, "built itself a cosmology out of what it could measure, out of what it could see and hear and smell and taste and feel. Anything which was not measurable was derided or ignored. Like all other cosmologies, this one was built of bricks which made a pleasing and consistent pattern, according to the tastes of time, and all other bricks were classified as unsuitable for construction purposes. Physical science, for instance, built a sturdy tower on Sir William Crookes's observations of X rays and ignored his equally authentic observation of levitation. And, like all other inflexible cosmologies, this one was doomed to attack from bricks denied admittance and internal decay.

"An analysis of its own bricks led physical science into regions where quantities lended themselves less and less readily to observation and measurement until, with such things as atomic research and uncertainty principles, today's cosmology becomes just as much a matter of faith as medieval Christianity. Dr. Rhine—"

"We've heard all this before, Kleinman," Frederickson grumbled. "Let's get on with it."

Kleinman's face hardened. "Very well." He took from one of the shelves a round, black, metallic cylinder about four inches in diameter and three inches high. He handed it around for inspection. "You will notice that this is nothing but a pedestal with a light source operated by battery."

Burris passed it to Dean. He looked it over curiously. The metal was thin. Inside was a small light bulb and a dry cell battery. Dean passed it on.

"I invite you to inspect the table," Kleinman said. "It is nothing more than an old telephone table which I had covered for greater effect."

They looked at each other. Finally Phil stepped forward, knocked on the top, peered underneath at the bottom, and stepped back. From a cabinet beneath one of the shelves, Kleinman removed a glass sphere. It seemed filled with small white balls.

"This globe," Kleinman said, "blown to my order, was filled with marbles before it was sealed. All of them except one are white. The odd one is black. You will notice that there is no way—no physical way—to remove any of the marbles without breaking the globe."

He handed the sphere carefully to Frederickson. The chemistry chairman snorted and passed it on. The sphere was about eight inches in diameter and packed almost solid with marbles.

Dean was surprised at its weight when he held it in his hands. He looked at it, puzzled. It reminded him of something. He shrugged and handed it to Phil.

Kleinman placed the metal cylinder in the center of the table and switched on the little light. When the sphere reached him, he placed it on top of the cylinder. Dean smothered a chuckle. Of course. Sitting there, the sphere looked like a penny ball-gum machine. Put in a penny and get a ball of gum. Except you'd have trouble getting the black one. It was right at the top.

Kleinman switched off the overhead light. The only illumination in the room was the light filtering through the marbles in the glass sphere. Everyone's face became suddenly changed and rather horrible in the light and shadow. Dean thought they all looked like witches peering over a flickering caldron or — more aptly — like fortune tellers reading the future in a crystal ball.

Burris jumped when the lights went off. "Is this mumbo-jumbo necessary?" he protested.

Kleinman turned from a door leading out of the library. It was not the one they had entered. "A physician of not-so-many-years ago would think modern asepsis mumbo-jumbo," he said dryly. "All experiments have their necessary conditions."

He opened the door. The room beyond was dimly lit. "Willy," he said. "Willy!"

Kleinman was little better than a silhouette in the doorway. Beside him appeared another silhouette that did not reach to his shoulder.

"Yes?" answered the sullen, high-pitched voice Dean remembered.

The little shadow seemed to flinch in the doorway and draw back. The big shadow almost dragged him into the room. When they got into the light, Dean saw that Willy was a boy, perhaps thirteen or fourteen years old, with tangled black hair that fell over his forehead. Below dark eyebrows were small, burning eyes that shifted uneasily and suspiciously around the room.

The boy was thin, and his face was pointed. He reminded Dean of a small, meat-eating animal, a weasel, perhaps. He looked hungry; he looked as if he would never get enough to eat.

"This is Willy," Kleinman said proudly. "As far as he knows he has no last name, but it doesn't matter. Willy is a very unusual boy with quite surprising powers. In a few months, I think, he will have no need of a last name."

They stared at Willy as if he were something on exhibit. Kleinman led Willy to the chair and half-helped, half-forced him down into it. Willy's eyes never stopped moving around the room. In the light of the marble-filled sphere he looked scarcely human, more animal than ever—or perhaps something else, for which there was an emotion but no name.

Kleinman went back and closed the door. The room was silent. Willy crouched on his chair as if he was about to spring at them or away from them as fear spurred him.

"It is not necessary that Willy be present in the room," Kleinman said, "but I thought you would all be happier to have the agency of the action in front of you. The demonstration will consist of this: Willy will teleport the black marble—the black marble alone, mind you—from the inside of the globe to the outside. This should demonstrate the selectivity of the power. Afterwards you will have further opportunity to inspect all the equipment. Unlike a magician, I have placed nothing here to distract you. Keep your eyes on the black marble. You will see it disappear from the globe while you are watching it. Is everything understood? Are there any complaints about the conditions of the demonstration?"

His face looked white and priestlike in the distorted light.

Phil leaned over and put his lips close to Dean's ear. "There's your ferret," he whispered. Dean suppressed a start.

"All right," Frederickson said impatiently. "Let's get on with it." His voice sounded strained and distant.

The room was quiet except for someone's deep breathing.

"Go ahead, Willy," Kleinman said softly.

The black marble looked up at them from diffused whiteness like an unblinking pupil.

Dean stared at the marble for a few moments. Nothing happened to it. He glanced at Willy. The boy was leaning forward in his chair, his eyes closed. His face was tight and more pointed than ever. Dean could almost feel the boy's mind working, boiling in his skull, reaching out with intangible fingers to grasp the black marble and lift it through some not-space to the outside.

Dean shivered.

He looked at Kleinman. The psychologist was gazing fixedly at Willy, his lips working soundlessly.

On Dean's right, Burris swayed forward. He was staring at the black marble, his face screwed up in concentration. His face and his head, a mottled white, were beaded with sweat.

Next to Burris, Frederickson's long face seemed pulled in upon itself, as if it were all going to be drawn up and projected through his eyes, which did not waver from the black marble. Absently, he drew the back of his hand across his forehead.

Past Frederickson the expressions of the others were indistinguishable. Dean turned his head to the left. Phil—even Phil—was straining forward, his eyes on the sphere.

It felt hot and stuffy in the room. The silence became unbearable. The tension mounted.

Dean wanted to do something, say something. He wanted to shout, *What's the matter with everybody?* But he didn't. He knew what was the matter with everybody.

They're afraid. They're afraid of this fourteen-year-old boy with the ferret face. They're afraid he can really do this impossible thing. They're afraid he really has this terrible power and can control it. They won't ever admit it, but they're afraid.

How can you trust a ferret? Dean thought. *How can you trust a hungry ferret? You train a ferret to chase rabbits out of their burrows or carry lines through pipes. But what if he decides not to chase the rabbit? What if he bites through his muzzle and escapes through a hole that only he can find? And he is loose, with his unappeasable hunger among the chicken runs of the world.*

But it's not that. Dean decided. *That's only part of it. It's not just Willy; it's anyone. A ferret doesn't eat its prey; he sucks its blood. This kind of ferret could suck the life from a whole system of ideas, and they would collapse, white, lifeless.*

What would these men do with a force they could not measure? What would they do with an effect they could not duplicate?

They were fighting for the world they knew, for sanity, for order in the universe. They were battling chaos. They were fighting for their lives.

How can you pen in something that is stronger than you are? How can you keep imprisoned forces you cannot even admit, against which you have no defense? You can't trust a ferret.

There was only one answer. *There are no ferrets.*

Dean felt strangely relieved. He let out his breath and realized he had been holding it and breathed deeply. He sneaked a glance at his watch. Only two minutes had elapsed. He remembered the time he had taken a swimming test which required that he stay afloat for five minutes. Five minutes. That's not a very long time. But he couldn't float, and after a few minutes of treading water he thought he understood what made people throw up their arms and sink rather than struggle any longer.

Out of the corner of his eye Dean saw something flicker. It was the black marble. It moved. He looked directly at it, and it moved again. But it was still there. Still in the glass sphere.

He stared at it. His heart beat faster. His breath came quick and harsh. His hands and feet got cold and then hot. Something trickled down the side of his neck and under his collar.

I'm afraid, he thought wonderingly. *I'm afraid, too.*

He concentrated on the black marble. *Don't move,* he willed. *Don't move! There are no ferrets!*

The battle continued and drew out unendurably. Dean sneaked a glance at Willy. The boy's face was screwed up in agony of effort.

Quickly Dean switched his eyes back to the marble.

A moment later the boy broke. He screamed. "I can't I can't I can't I can't...."

Frederickson snorted. "Let's end this farce." He took two swift steps to the wall switch and flicked on the overhead light.

Someone laughed nervously. Someone else joined in. Then everybody was laughing. It was hard to stop.

"Please," Kleinman was begging. "Please. Just a few minutes more. I'm sure the boy can do it. He's done it dozens of times before. You've got to give him another chance. I've got records. I can show you...."

Burris led the way out of the room. Kleinman followed. As Dean left he looked back at the boy in the chair. Willy was slumped, boneless, his eyes closed.

There are no ferrets.

The gaiety in the living room was almost feverish. Kleinman had left. No one would listen to him. Burris was chuckling happily.

"The look on his face! Fabulous! 'Keep your eye on the black marble!'"

"I hope," Frederickson said piously, "that this experience will straighten him out."

"And yet," Dean muttered, almost to himself, "I would have sworn that the marble moved."

Burris picked it up instantly. "Nonsense. Optical illusion. Stare at anything that long and apparent movement is inevitable."

Everyone nodded. Emphatically. Dean went to find his coat. As he reached the door, Kleinman rushed past him into the room.

"Has anyone seen Willy?" he asked frantically.

Everyone looked at him blankly.

"He's gone," Kleinman went on. His glance darted around the room as if he suspected one of the others of concealing him. "He's not in his room. I've searched the house."

"Maybe he stepped out for a breath of air," someone suggested and started to laugh. He stopped abruptly.

"But he can't be gone," Kleinman said, his eyes almost horrified. "The doors are both bolted on the inside. He has to be in the house."

He turned and started away at a trot. Dean looked after him for a moment and went into the hall. His cost was hanging in a closet. He took it off the hanger.

Somewhere a phone was ringing. Dean stopped, thought, and remembered. In the library.

He opened the door. Empty of people the room looked different. The glass sphere resting whitely on its pedestal was no longer a threat. It was futility. The phone on the floor kept on ringing, louder and insistent.

Dean walked to the corner and picked up the phone, cradle and all.

"Hello?" He set the cradle down on the velvet-covered table.

"Mr. Simpson?" The voice sounded thin and distant.

"Yes." His voice shook a little.

"This is the hospital calling for Dr. Hendricks. Your wife's breathing has become irregular. With your permission, the doctor has decided to operate."

Dean put a hand on the table to steady himself. Something pressed into his palm. Unconsciously, he picked it up and clenched it in his fist.

"Mr. Simpson, did you hear me?"

"Yes. Go on."

"Before proceeding with an operation of this nature, Dr. Hendricks wishes to have your written consent."

"Of course," Dean said with difficulty.

"If you will come to the hospital as soon as possible, we will prepare your wife for surgery...."

The voice went on, threadily, in his ear, but Dean couldn't think clearly any more.

Mary! he thought in anguish.

His hand was hurting him. He unclenched it. He rolled it back and forth in his palm...

PART II

To Diana and Karen

INTRODUCTION

The first half of The *Unpublished Gunn* ended with "The Black Marble" and the Gunn family on its way back to Kansas City for my second try at full-time writing. We had lived for a few weeks with my wife's parents in Chanute and then in an upstairs apartment in a two-story house, which my three-year-old son Kit called "the department." In Kansas City my brother, who is a physician, had bought a house and our parents had moved in with him, so we had the use of my parent's bungalow rent-free. That and the prospect of free medical care removed a great deal of the pressure of earning a living with my typewriter.

The failure of "The Black Marble" and "The Whip" to find a sympathetic editor removed some of the glow from the success of "The Man Who Owned Tomorrow" and "Wherever You May Be," the short story and the novella that I had written in Chanute, after my trip to New York. I interrupted my freelancing career to take a job with City Hall as assistant director of civil defense. Then a contract arrived from my agent, Fred Pohl, for my first novel.

A company named Abelard was starting up an SF line and had accepted the fifty pages and outline of *This Fortress World,* a novel I had started a year before while working as a paperback editor in Racine. It was only $500, but it was a contract and a novel, and I quit my job of three months to pick up where I had left off.

I equipped a basement study in my brother's house and spent eight hours a day there, writing ten pages a day, revising once, and sending the stories out to find a home. It was a good time in our lives—not the most affluent certainly but a time of hope and productivity. I wrote two novels—*This Fortress World*, which I eventually took away from Abelard and sold to Gnome Books when Abelard wanted to edit it radically, and *Star Bridge*, with Jack Williamson. Jack had started a novel some years before but got stuck with it. After we met at the Chicago World Convention of 1952, he asked me if I'd like to take it over, and I wrote it from his 150 pages of notes and 50-page beginning.

Although both novels have been reprinted frequently and profitably, both here and abroad, they seemed like financial mistakes at the time. I spent three months on each of them and at the time they earned only their advances of $500, and I split the advance for *Star Bridge* with Jack. That's when I developed what I later called Gunn's Law: Sell it twice. Novels seldom were serialized, so Gunn's Law meant that novel ideas were broken into shorter segments publishable in magazines as novelettes or short novels and then brought together as novels. That's the way I wrote *Station in Space. The Immortals,* and *The Joy Makers,* as well as a couple of later novels. The three parts of *The Joy Makers* were written during this period and all but the last of the four sections of *The Immortals* and the last two of the six sections of *Station in Space.*

I also wrote some 30 stories there and sold almost all of them to the magazines, although some took a year or two to find the right editor, and a couple of them took 15 years. It was success. Not wealth, for sure: I averaged about $3,000 a year for those two-and-a-half years, but each year was better than the one before, and eventually those stories would be reprinted in collections, anthologies, and novels and the income from them would be several times what it was at the time. That was one of the problems with freelancing in the early 1950s: writing was like depositing money in the bank. Eventually it would pay everything back with interest, but at the time it felt like living from mail delivery to mail delivery.

My acceptance rate may have led me to try the slick magazines. My thirty-fifth story, "Jackpot for Julie," was the result. My analysis of slick-magazine fiction had suggested that I had the best chance with the light romantic story, but the only thing I got from "Jackpot for Julie," my forty-second story, "The Man with One Talent," and my forty-fifth story, "The Big One," were some kind rejection slips, particularly from an associate editor at *Collier's*.

In 1955 we moved back to Lawrence, Kansas, where my wife and I had both attended the University of Kansas. We liked Lawrence as a place to live and a place to bring up children. We had two sons now, Kit, nearly six, and Kevin, a year old. Although I didn't know it, my full-time writing days were over until after my retirement in 1993. Within a month I had been asked by the chairman of the English Department to teach a couple of classes, and before the end of the fall semester the executive secretary of the Alumni Association had asked me to edit the Alumni publications.

Teaching and editing were both part-time jobs, and I got some writing done. While I was working for the Alumni Association, particularly, I took off a week each month and a couple of months in the summer when I wrote "Powder Keg" and "Space Is a Lonely Place," which completed *Station in Space* and started my four-book publishing career with Bantam Books, through the efforts of the agent who had succeeded Fred Pohl, Harry Altshuler.

"Powder Keg" was particularly important because I wrote it in a writers workshop I took with Carolyn Gordon. It was the only class in fiction writing I had taken and Carolyn convinced me not only that there was much I didn't know about writing but that fiction writing could be taught. I think my work after that was more knowledgeable about the craft.

During this period I also wrote "The Immortals," which became the final short novel that made up *The Immortals*. Bantam published *Stations in Space* in 1958, *The Joy Makers,* in 1961, *The Immortals,* in 1962, and a collection of short stories, *Future Imperfect,* in 1964.

About the time I was working on "Space Is a Lonely Place" the thought occurred to me that if I couldn't sell non-SF short stories to the slicks, I might be able to sell them SF. Robert Heinlein, Ray Bradbury, Robert Sheckley, and others had been able to do that. Some of my earlier stories had that kind of ambition, "The Cave of Night," for instance, which Harry Altshuler had tried only at *Collier's* before sending it over to *Galaxy*. My only success with the slicks had been "The Man Who Owned Tomorrow." What distinguished "slick" SF from that in the SF magazines, I decided, was a more general theme, a setting in the not-too-distant future, and an idea that did not present serious difficulties for an unsophisticated readership.

I wrote a couple of stories aimed at that market. One of them, my sixty-first, "The House Dutiful," I later revised as "The Technological Revolution" for Bob Hoskins's *Infinity Two* anthology. Then came the final short story I didn't sell, my sixty-fourth, "Pest House."

In 1958 I was hired by the University as administrative assistant to the Chancellor for University Relations, where I spent twelve years, most of them too busy for writing. Then, toward the end of that period, I began taking the month of vacation I had earned and devoting it to fiction. I finished the last two short novels, "Trial by Fire" and "Witch Hunt," for *If* and *Galaxy* and the book that became *The Burning*. I also write "The Listeners," the first of the six novelettes that became *The Listeners,* and the second chapter of what later became *Kampus*.

By 1970 I had decided to return to teaching full-time and a second career. For me teaching and writing formed a productive combination that resulted in two books a year for a while, including *The Witching Hour, Breaking Point, Some Dreams Are Nightmares, The End of the Dreams, The Magicians, Alternate Worlds: The Illustrated History of Science Fiction*, the four volumes of *The Road to Science Fiction, The Dreamers, Isaac Asimov: The Foundations of Science Fiction, Crisis!*, and *The New Encyclopedia of Science Fiction*.

But that is another story. The days of unpublished stories were over. I hope.

James Gunn
Lawrence, Kansas

THE WHIP

Why do men go north?

The forest path was narrow but well defined.

On either side the trees and bushes were green and chaotic, rich with the color and odor of late-blooming flowers and ripening berries, filled with the aimless stirrings of life. The wildness and the chill, winy air was an unexpected contrast to the tamed uniformity of the garden communities of the south.

A few disordered thoughts filtered through to Jason's consciousness.

As he walked slowly toward his unknown destination, a rabbit flopped out of a bush ahead, stared fearlessly at him for a moment, and hopped away. Far to the right a single bird was singing. Jason listened.

The whip whistled as it cut through the air. Jason's head came up. His back arched. His knees sagged and almost buckled from the exquisite pain. He strangled a groan in his throat.

What am I doing here? he thought blindly. *Why am I being whipped?*

Nothing in his forty years of life had prepared him for the agony that flooded his body and washed away all reality but this. Life was freedom. Freedom to do as one pleased. One must respect another's freedom or lose his own. Freedom is indivisible. All are free or none.

I am not being beaten, he thought defiantly. *No one has the right to beat me.*

Again the whip fell upon his bare back. Unarguable refutation. Jason staggered, but some unconscious determination kept him moving forward along the path.

Why am I being whipped? Who is whipping me?

He did not look back. He was afraid to look. His thoughts turned and twisted feverishly, trying to reconcile the unreconcilable.

Life is not pain. No one has the right to whip me. The whip is imaginary. The pain is imaginary. I am mad.

And again.

Life is not pain. This is death. Death.

The pain began to ebb....

Death sat in the corner of the room. It sat in its accustomed niche, in the ritual cup, waiting for him. Jason studied it. He had only to fill the cup with water and drink it down. Death would be almost instantaneous. The ultimate freedom.

A gently mellow note disturbed the air. Jason turned and considered the two buttons on the desk, a white one and a black one. He pressed the white one.

"I beg permission to disturb your privacy," said the door.

"Enter," said Jason.

The door swung open. The short fat man with the gray hair took one step into the room and stopped. He lowered his eyes to the floor.

"You are sure that I do not intrude."

"You do not intrude," Jason said. His firm lips twisted. *Formality.* As bone-deep as it was, sometimes it sickened him.

Micah settled himself with a sigh into a large chair. Jason glanced once more at the death cup and then turned to face his guest.

"Your work is finished?" Micah asked heavily.

"Finished," Jason said flatly. He stood feet spread apart, hands clasped behind him, tall and broad shouldered, but his dark, graying head was bent forward and his eyes stared at the floor. "The machine you found, Micah—the ship—has been cleaned, studied, renewed. The rust has been removed. The instruments and controls have been traced and analyzed. Tall, slim, poised, it stands in the desert—a monument. Twenty years of work, finished."

"No fuel?"

Jason shook his head. "Unless you have news," he said. Looking up.

Micah sighed. "No. You are sure that it is the heavy, unstable metal we need?"

"It breaks down," Jason said. "A small amount of matter becomes a great deal of energy—the energy we need to propel the ship into space. We can't get enough any other way. And we found traces in the fuel chamber. And lead. It breaks down into lead."

"But it is so rare," Micah said. "Why should they use a fuel that is so scarce?"

"They?"

"The ones who built the ship."

"Men," Jason said, his dark eyes brooding. "It was built for men like us. I have sat in their chairs and worked their controls with my two hands. I have climbed their ladders and lain in their beds. I have looked into their mirrors and seen them looking out at me."

"You are more certain than our philosophers," Micah commented drily.

Jason shrugged. "I have lived closer to them."

"Where did they go, then?"

Jason waved a hand toward the ceiling. "Out there, perhaps, where we would like to go. Or perhaps they are here."

"Here?"

"In this room."

Micah chuckled. "You and me? Oh, no, Jason. Could we have lived in their swarming cities when they were new? We never gather in groups of more than three or four, and we are most at ease when alone. No, Jason. You must explain me that and explain why we have no memory of them, no record. Explain why the past ends a few hundred years ago, and explain the ruins and why we never go there. Then I may believe you."

"It does not matter," Jason said. "It I could explain those things, perhaps I could explain why we can find no fuel metal. Perhaps they need it because nothing else would work."

"But there is none," Micah complained, "none at all. Volunteers have searched the civilized world and brought back nothing."

"Have they searched the ruins?" Jason asked.

"Of course not!" Micah looked surprised. "You know that it is psychologically impossible for us to enter the ruins."

Psychologically impossible! Jason sighed. It was psychologically impossible for me to do many things. To mingle in large groups. To force another to do something he does not want to do. To surrender one's freedom.

"Have any gone north?" Jason asked.

Micah's eyes narrowed. About many things he was very shrewd. "One. Theron. You remember him. He has been gone almost sixty days now. He thought he was on the trail of something, but he would not tell me what it was."

"Sixty days," Jason mused. His eyes drifted to the ritual cup. "Then he will not return."

Micah followed Jason's gaze. "I said that my volunteers brought back nothing. That is not quite true. They brought back information which made me wish, fleetingly, for some kind of central agency for gathering data. It was very curious. A student of psychology might make much of it."

Jason's eyes drifted back to Micah.

"Two persons out of every ten," Micah said softly, "drink death from the ritual cups."

Jason's eyebrows lifted. "So many?"

Micah nodded. "Two more go into lifetime seclusion. One out of ten disappears. Completely. He is presumed to have gone north."

"North? Why north?"

"Yes," Micah said. "Why? Why do men go north?"

"The flagellants?" Jason suggested.

"Perhaps," Micah said, frowning. "But some that have disappeared from our community—I would not have thought them likely prospects for the Prophet. Yet, who can say?"

Jason's patience broke. "Will you order me to go north?"

"Order?" Micah echoed in amazement. "Of course not."

"That is what you have been hinting at. If you order me to go, I will go. Otherwise—" His eyes turned toward the niche in the corner. "My work is finished."

"You know that I cannot order you to go," Micah said softly. "But before you do anything final, think of your wife"—Jason frowned—"and your son." The frown deepened. "Why should anyone drink from the cup," Micah went on, "when life is so pleasant?" He shook his head. "Two out of ten! Five out of ten!"

After Micah left, Jason stared at the ritual cup for a long time. *Jeri! Dion!*

And yet— He lifted his head.

Why do men go north?

Something touched Jason's back. He flinched, waiting for the whip to strike. Nothing happened. He turned. The whip was extended toward him, butt first. Dazedly he closed his hand over it. The other slipped past him. Their bare shoulders brushed. Jason stared at the whip.

It was made of leather. It was about four feet long. The butt fitted solidly in his hand. There were three lashes. Knotted into them were small pieces of jagged metal. The lashes were dark, almost black, except where they were freshly stained with blood. His blood.

Something trickled down his back. He could not take his eyes off the whip.

Impatiently the other moved off down the path. Without volition Jason started after him. As Jason lifted his eyes, the back twitched.

The other was a young man. He seemed scarcely older than Dion. But his back was ridged with old scars and blue cuts crusted with dried blood. The skin stretched tautly across the ribs. From his waist hung unrecognizable rags. His feet were bare.

The back twitched again. Dimly Jason remembered what he was supposed to do. He raised the whip. As he brought it down the strength flowed out of his arm like water. The lashes curled harmlessly around the young man's shoulders.

The back twitched it off, irritated, as if the lashes were insects.

Gritting his teeth, Jason raised the whip again. He brought it down. The flesh split. Blood welled around the bits of metal. Jason felt sick.

Dion, my son, he thought. *Dion. Dion.*

He raised the whip....

Dion lolled in a sunken tub of blood-warm water. He reached for the frosted glass on the floor, but the boy was quicker. He picked it up and placed it in Dion's hand.

"Thank you, Clare," Dion said lazily. He nodded toward the door. "Will you wait for me?"

The boy's delicate skin reddened. His dark eyes flashed hatred at Jason as he turned away.

"These are new amusements," Jason said heavily when the boy was gone.

"Aren't they," Dion agreed. It seemed almost too much effort for him to speak. "But then, what have we to do except amuse ourselves? Does it matter, as long as we interfere with no one else?"

"That is the new philosophy?" Jason asked.

"New? Oh, no, it is old. But we have not had the leisure until now. Your grandfather did his work well." Dion smiled. "Dear great-grandfather Samson, he tamed the sun for us. He harnessed it to our needs, and we no longer have to work. A house? Spray it in a few hours. Power? Great-grandfather Samson's solar engine on the roof. Food? A few hours a week tending the hydroponics." He stretched, lazily. "The rest of the time we must amuse ourselves as best we can."

"That, it seems to me, is self-defeating," Jason said. "Eventually you will run out of amusements. What will you do then?"

"There will always be something new."

"You think there is when you are young," Jason said softly. "But you will grow old, and the world will grow old with you. What will you do then?"

Dion shrugged. "I will face that problem when I come to it—if I come to it."

"Two out of ten," Jason said reminiscently, "drink death from the ritual cups. Two go into seclusion. One disappears. Which will you choose, Dion?"

"What of the other five?" Dion asked.

Jason looked around the room. The lush, scarlet matting on the floor; the purple grapes; the deep chairs. He felt out of place and depressed. He had never cared for social bathing. "Yes, what of them?" Was their choice any better—or any different?

"What would you have me do, father?" Dion asked. "Waste my life as you have wasted yours? Throw myself into something which is doomed from the start? Oh, everyone knows you have found no fuel. They knew it was folly a long time ago. The last five years you have worked alone."

"At least," Jason said, "I had twenty years with something I believed in. What do you believe in?"

"Pleasure," Dion said. "There are so many different kinds. Physical pleasure, mental pleasure, creative pleasure. Like that, for instance." He swung an arm lazily at the wall behind Jason.

Jason got up and looked. It was a square of plastic pressed in place against the wall. Jason's first reaction was that Dion had talent; he had always done well at anything he tried. Lately — Jason had been shocked at the change in him.

The picture was well planned, imaginatively composed, skillfully executed. But there was something horribly wrong with it.

In the foreground of the picture was a naked girl, slim, beautiful, desirable, against a background of gray desert and close-hanging gray clouds. She was bent forward from the waist. Across her back was a long welt, red against the whiteness of her skin. Lashing out from a cloud hand was a black, vicious whip. And on the girl's face was a look of surrender, of ecstasy, of almost sexual passion.

"Do you like it?" Dion asked.

"No," Jason said flatly. "It looks like Avis."

"It is Avis."

Jason stared at his son. "What do you mean?"

A muscle quivered in Dion's jaw, but he went on casually. "Avis has gone north. She heard the Prophet predict the end of the world, and she has gone north for a mass purification. She preferred the flagellants to becoming my wife." Dion's face was expressionless; his tone was flat.

Jason stared, unbelieving. "And you let her go?"

"Of course," Dion said. "She is free to do as she wishes, just as I am. How could I stop her? Why should I want to?"

"You let her go north to be whipped?" Jason said incredulously. "To have her back cut into quivering ribbons until she drops...."

"You intrude!" Dion snapped flushing.

"I cannot intrude," Jason shouted. "I am your father."

Dion stood up in the tub and stepped out onto the floor, dripping. He faced Jason proudly. "I am eighteen. You intrude." He turned away. He went to the dryer and stood before it.

Jason stared at Dion's back. His body was strong and tall and unblemished. He had inherited that from Jason.

"What is wrong with our race?" Jason said, almost to himself.

"What do you mean?" Dion asked defiantly. "There is nothing wrong with it. We have freedom and leisure. What more can you ask?"

"I don't know. The will to live? I didn't notice it before, but I wonder how the race has survived this long." Jason stood still, thinking. "North, you said? Why do men go north? Dion," he said humbly, "will you go north with me to find Theron? He went to search for my fuel metal and has not returned."

"No, father."

"Will you go with me to find Avis?"

"No, father."

Jason went to Dion and took his hand. "Please, Dion," he said.

Dion disengaged his hand. "Clare is waiting," he said. Smiling, he glanced at the picture on the wall before he turned away.

Jason looked at it once more. The whip seemed to move....

The whip faltered in the air. There was nothing for it to strike. The path was empty in front of Jason. He swayed on his feet and almost fell.

Then he saw it, crumpled at the edge of the path. It looked like an old red rag, tattered. It did not move. Jason decided, vaguely, that it would not move again.

The thought penetrated. He had killed a man. He had whipped a man to death. Jason vomited into the bushes. When he straightened up, his head was a little clearer.

What am I doing here? Why have I killed a man?

He could not remember the answers. Was that the mystery? He wondered. Were those the unanswerable questions?

He felt disembodied. Somewhere, far away, there was something that was stiff, that ached, dully, eternally. It did not matter. It was too far away to matter.

His feet started to carry him, stumbling, down the path. *Where am I going?* He thought. He did not know the answer to that question either. He stopped thinking about it. He stopped thinking at all.

He plodded forward, the whip dangling forgotten from one hand.

He came back to awareness with a sensation of pain. It was dark now, and it was raining. The water was trickling into the cuts on his back. His back felt like a solid mass of fire.

He was still standing. His face was pressed against something hard and rough. His body had wedged itself into a kind of partial shelter, but his back was unprotected. If it were not for his back, the cool rain would feel good. His face was hot; his body was burning. And then he started to shiver.

He knew what he was facing now. It was a door, a crude kind of door. He fumbled at it.

"Go away!"

He looked up, his eyes unfocused. Had someone said something or was it in his mind? He fumbled again with the door.

The door swung open. He faced a square of light. He blinked. Warmth crept out toward him.

"Go away!" the light said. "Why do you keep coming? Why do you keep bothering me? I don't want anything to do with any of you."

Jason raised one hand uncertainly to shade his eyes. It was the hand with the whip in it.

"Oh, I see," the light said scornfully. "You've beaten your partner to death, and you want someone to take his place. Well,

I won't whip you, and I certainly won't let you whip me. Goon! You'll find plenty of others farther on. Go away and die!"

Jason nodded, or thought he did. He understood now. He was intruding.

He turned and started off into the night. For a little way the light from the doorway lit up the path and then it was gone. He tripped in the darkness and then his knees went limp. He pitched forward, face down in the mud.

Someone was pulling at him. He had been very peaceful. Someone was turning him over. The rain, cold against his face, shocked his eyes open. A face was bending over him, a woman's face.

"Jeri," he said. His voice was so weak that he could scarcely hear it. "Jeri..."

The weeds had come back. The lawn was almost indistinguishable. The trees had edged closer, too, and the vines. They crawled up the sides of the house, smothering it, working at it. Even the colorful plastic seemed dimmed by age. The isolation that the garden community emphasized had almost done its work too well.

Jason remembered when the house was new, when the lawn was green and perfect. He remembered when he had first brought Jeri to the house. They had been young then. They had been young together.

"Do you think," Jeri had said eagerly, "do you think they could have had anything as beautiful as this before?"

"Before when?"

"Before whatever happened that made the ruins."

"Do you think they were like us?"

"Oh, yes," Jeri had said. "Only not as wise and not as much in love." She had glanced at him, alive with promise. "I think they were just like us, and they did something very bad and then they were punished. We won't ever be bad, will we, Jason?"

"Never. And I'm sure they never had anything as beautiful." But he had been staring at Jeri.

She had smiled and slipped her hand into his and they went up to the door. It had opened before them. Hand in hand, they had entered their new home. The door had closed behind. Jeri had twirled, ecstatically.

"We will live here forever," she had said. "We will never leave. Everything we will ever want is here."

She had thrown herself into his arms and they had been happy. Everything they had wanted was there. For a time, it had been true.

But Jason left to pursue his dream. It had caused their first quarrel. *How can you leave me?*

And their second quarrel. *It's madness. Surely you can't be serious about going millions of miles away!*

And the third. *It's foolish. It's silly. It will never work.*

And the others that had come and shed their tears and gone away almost as if they had never been. Almost, but not quite.

Dion had been born and for years Jeri was preoccupied with him. But Dion had left, too. Jason had left and Dion had left, but Jeri had never left. Jeri had stayed.

The house was depressing. Jason decided that he should not have come. Why had he come? To tell Jeri— To tell Jeri what? To tell Jeri that he was going north where no one lived, where the ruins were, where the sun did not shine enough to supply a house's power needs, where a searcher after a rare metal had disappeared, where a girl was being whipped on by a lash from the sky?

How could he tell Jeri? He did not know himself why he was going. Was he searching for a lode of a heavy, unstable metal that would power a dream-ship? Was he hunting for a lost man who had vanished on a mission for him? Was he chasing a lost girl his son had loved?

Or was it all this? Was it this and something more? Was he seeking the answer to a question he could not even frame?

Where did we come from? Why are we sick? Why does the past end a few hundred years ago?

Why do men go north?

How could he tell Jeri? Jason knew he could not tell Jeri. He had come here, as he had come before, in search of someone who was lost, lost long ago, someone who would never be found.

Jason stepped in front of the door. The door did not open, as it had not opened years before.

"Jeri will not see anyone," the door said, as it had said then. "No one will be admitted. Do not intrude."

"I am Jason," he said.

"Jeri will not see anyone," the door repeated. "No...."

Suddenly forty years of civilization slipped away. He pounded on the door. "Jeri," he shouted. "Jeri!"

The only answer came from the door. "Jeri will not see...."

Jason turned away. It was futile. The door would keep on until he left. This is the way it had been years before. He had come home, unsuspecting, and the door would not open.

How many years has it been? he thought. *Five years? Six?*

Others had shut themselves away. Others had cut themselves off from the world. Two out of ten, Micah had said. But he had never thought that Jeri would shut herself up, that she would shut him away from her.

He could force his way into the house, but he shuddered at the thought.

Perhaps she is dead. It has been a long time. She might very well be dead. He thought of her as being dead. It did not disturb him.

As he walked away from the clearing that was disappearing into the forest it had been carved from, he knew that he would never come back. Jeri was dead.

Good-by, Jeri....

He came back to life slowly. A coolness was on his forehead. It felt good. He lay there for a little, savoring his return from death. He opened his eyes.

"Jeri," he said, but he knew he was being foolish. Jeri had been blond. This girl was dark-haired and young—only a little older than Dion—and beautiful in a wild, untamed way. Perhaps that is what had misled him. She was as beautiful as Jeri had been.

The odor of something delicious made his mouth water. He could not remember the last time he had eaten.

The coolness was lifted from Jason's forehead. Jason sniffed.

"Here," the girl said. "Eat."

Jason opened his mouth. The girl put a spoon to his lips. Jason let the warm broth trickle down his throat. It was delicious. He tried to raise himself a little higher.

A groan broke from his throat.

"Lie still," she said.

Jason lay still. She fed him broth until the bowl was empty. While she went to put the bowl away, Jason looked around the room. It was small and bare and crude.

The walls had been hand fashioned out of wood. The floor was the same. The chairs and a table had been sawed and fitted together with pegs and laced with rope. An open fire was laid in a stone opening against one wall. Jason stared at it. He had not seen an open fire for a long time.

There was something wrong about the room. Jason puzzled about it for a moment and then gave up.

He was lying in a bunk built against one wall. It was the only bunk. Jason wondered where the girl had slept.

The girl was back. She was not so tall as Jeri had been. She seemed sturdier and curved where Jeri had been slim. Even in a rough-woven cloth shirt and pants she looked very desirable.

"Turn over," she said.

Jason tried to turn, but the pain in his back stopped him midway. He fell back.

"Try again," she said. "I'll help."

He tried again. She helped him with an arm that seemed strong and capable. He lay on his stomach.

She pulled a covering of cloth from his back. He winced as it stuck to his flesh.

Something liquid trickled on his back. It burned for a moment and then was cool. She rubbed it in. After a moment his back began to feel better. It lost some of its stiffness, and her hand felt gently sensual rubbing it.

"How did you get mixed up with them?" she asked.

He turned his head to look at her. "How do you know I'm not one of them?"

"You've never been beaten before," she said. "I've seen them. Too many of them. Their backs are masses of ridges. Besides," — she smiled at him—"you talked while you were feverish. They never talk. They don't even groan."

"What did I say?"

"You kept mumbling questions."

"What questions?"

"'Why am I being whipped?' you said. And over and over again, 'Why do men go north?'"

Jason laughed harshly. "Did I answer them?" She shook her head. "Do you know the answers?" he asked.

"Do you?"

He looked at her sharply and then around the room. Definitely, there was something wrong with it.

"I know the answer to one of them," he said. His eyes clouded over as if with pain. He remembered....

The helicopter had taken him a long way, but it reached the edge of the power beams and settled to the earth like a winged seed.

After finding the other helicopter, locating the trail was easy. The path led north.

The forest was different here. There were more elms and beeches and maples; they grew thick and wild. And the air was much cooler than anything he had ever known.

After the second day his food gave out. He hesitated at the edge of the path next morning. He had never been hungry before, not for long. Then he started off at a fast walk, wearing off the stiffness brought on by the unaccustomed exercise and the cold night. The path still led north.

By afternoon he was very tired. He was so tired that he had forgotten his hunger. He was walking slowly now. He wondered what he would do for food and shelter. It was getting too cold to sleep in the bushes.

Food was more important. He supposed that there were ways of getting food. Man had not always had hydroponics. There were animals in the forest. He had seen them. Rabbits. Raccoons. A deer. They were unafraid. Perhaps he could lure a small one close enough to hit it with a stick, a rabbit, maybe. But how could he cook it. He had nothing with him to start a fire. Raw? He shuddered. Perhaps he might eat it raw, if he were hungry enough.

He didn't feel that hungry. He kept on walking. The sun was getting low in the west when he heard the sound.

He stopped and listened. The sound came again. It was faint and distant. It was like someone hitting a rotten log.

Jason began to run. Ahead the path bent, so that the forest looked like a solid green wall. But as he ran toward it, the wall broke and opened in front of him.

When he heard the sound again, it was closer. Jason rounded the corner. He saw the whip raised, slowly, methodically, and then brought down. The scene had a dreamlike unreality about it—the half-naked man walking ahead of him, his arm rising and falling like something mechanical, and everything so meaningless, so slow.

Jason kept running. His breath burned his throat, but he noticed it only as a distant discomfort. As he drew closer, he could see more. Beyond the man rose a shoulder and part of a back that looked small and slim and white, except where it was patterned with red. He saw a head with long brown hair, snarled now and unkempt, that tumbled down over the shoulders. The head hung forward on a slender neck, as if it could no longer hold itself up.

"Avis!" Jason called.

The head half-turned as if to listen, but the whip came down again. The head came upright for a moment and looked toward the north and then sank back forward to stare at the ground.

"Avis!" Jason screamed.

The head did not respond. The whip fell. Slowly, then, like a flower wilting, the head dropped and sank from sight. The man walked on a few steps and stopped, puzzled. Behind him in the path he left a small crumpled figure, pitiful and still. Dully, he turned back to look.

Jason slowed. He walked forward taking great sobbing breaths. She lay in the middle of the path, half on her side. She was bare to the waist. Below that were only a few rags. Her back was scarlet, like Dion's floor matting.

Jason knelt beside her. "Avis," he said softly. She did not stir. Jason turned her partly over.

Her face was peaceful instead of the mask of pain Jason had expected. Her eyes were gently closed. Jason put his ear to her mouth. She breathed. Her breath fluttered in her throat.

Jason picked her up. She was very small and light. He carried her off the path to a bed of old leaves. He put her down. He spread his coat under her and around her. He fastened it over her small breasts that beamed whitely in the shadows.

"Avis," he said again, kneeling beside her. It was useless. He stayed there on his knees for a moment, feeling futile.

After a while he got up and found a stream of running water. He tried to scoop some up in his hands, but it all trickled out before he got back. He took off his blouse then, and tore it up. He soaked the strips and carried them back. He squeezed water into the corner of her mouth, but she drank only a little. The rest he used to bathe her forehead and face.

She was small and helpless and innocent like a child. Jason crouched over her, his face grim. All night long, he kept her warm with his body.

She died just before the dawn.

Jason did not want to leave her there for the animals to find, but the ground was too hard to dig up with his hands. Finally he placed his coat over her and covered her with leaves, it was the best he could do.

He stood up, shivering, and realized for the first time that he was cold. He turned around to go back to the path. The man stood there, tall, thin, silent. Only his eyes moved; they followed Jason, doglike.

How long has he been standing there? Jason wondered. "Go away," he said.

The man did not move. Jason noticed that the whip still dangled from his hand, three lashes like obscene dark tails.

How did Avis find him? How did she find someone to beat her? And then he thought, *Or is there always someone who will beat you, if you want to be beaten?*

A hot bitter tide of anger rose in Jason's throat. "Go away!" he shouted.

The man stood where he was, his eyes watching as if he saw everything and understood nothing. Jason took two quick steps. He wrenched the whip from the man's hand. He drew it back and swung it viciously. The lashes opened long red cuts across the man's side and face.

"There!" Jason screamed. "How do *you* like to be whipped?"

Mutely, the man turned toward the path. This time the whip fell on his back. Jason noticed that the man's back was ridged with old scars.

They were in the path. Stolidly the man turned north. He plodded on. Jason's anger ebbed, he stopped. He let the whip fall to his side.

This is what he wants, Jason thought. *He wants to go north. He wants to be whipped north.*

The man stopped walking and slowly turned his head to look back over his shoulder.

Why do men go north?

Suddenly the answer to that question became vitally important. Jason knew that he had to find out. And there was only one way to find out.

He walked toward the man, raising the whip....

She asked the question he had not expected. "Why is the ship important—the machine for taking men to other worlds?"

Why is the ship important? "I don't suppose it is," he said slowly, "except to me. But wait a minute—that's wrong. It might make a difference to the race. If it were a beginning instead of an end." He turned his head to look at her. "It would be something different to attempt, something to conquer. When we first started working on the ship there were dozens of volunteers, but they drifted away until I was all alone. That's why we have to find some of the fuel-metal. We have to find enough to reach the next nearest deposit so that we can go on. We must expand to live. We must grow to survive. What is your name?" he asked unexpectedly.

"Diana."

"Do you understand, Diana?"

She shook her head. "Not entirely. I wouldn't care to leave Earth. But I can understand how it might be important."

"Why did you take me in?" Jason asked suddenly. He watched her face.

She did not change expression, but her fingers stopped working on his back for a moment. She looked away. "I had—reasons."

Something was wrong. She kept sliding away. "Where did you sleep last night?" he asked.

"On the floor," she said. "I'm used to sleeping anywhere."

He looked at her lips. They were full and red. The lower one trembled as he watched.

"There is no need to do that," he said slowly. "The bunk is wide enough for two."

He took her hand and pulled her down. She came unresisting. Her face bent over his. A lock of hair fell softly against his face. Their lips met. *It has been a long time*, Jason thought.

She stiffened and got up in one fluid motion.

She stood beside the bunk, breathing quickly.

Jason clenched his teeth. The abrupt movement had jarred his back. *It is not that*, he thought. *That is not what makes her strange.* Now that it was done, he regretted it. "Forgive me," he said. "I intrude. You shall have the bunk tonight. I shall sleep on the floor."

"You—" she said. "I brought you in here because—because I was sorry for you."

"Of course," Jason said. "I realize. I am twice your age."

"You don't understand," she said hotly. "You wanted me only because it was the convenient thing to do. Casually, like eating or drinking."

"We do not take such things so seriously—" Jason began. He struggled to a sitting position and tried to get up. "I intrude. I will leave."

She pushed him back. "Stay there! I know your kind. You don't take anything seriously. Everything is a game to amuse you for a moment. Nothing is worth fighting for or living for. But you can find plenty of reasons for dying."

He tried to get up again.

She forced him to lie down, her hands on his shoulders. Her dark hair fell down on either side of her face.

This is worse than being whipped, he thought. *She has not right to stop me if I wish to leave.*

"I'm not going to let you go out there to die," she said. "How would you eat? How would you keep warm? You're going to stay here until you're well."

She straightened up, defying him, her hands on her hips. Her eyes were bright and her cheeks were red. Suddenly the proper thing to do seemed unimportant. Why was she so determined?

"All right," he said, and smiled.

She sat down on the edge of the bunk. "Now turn over," she said. "You've hurt your back again."

Obediently, he turned over. It was easier to move. He decided that the activity had helped it rather than hurt, but he did not tell her that.

She rubbed his back for a moment. It made Jason drowsy. "My mother," she said, "died when I was still a little girl. My father wept. It is one of my clearest memories. Afterwards he held me close and told me that he did not regret anything. They had lived, he said, a lifetime in a few years. Last year my father died. He went among the flagellants. They killed him. They whipped him to death. They never said a word."

"What was he doing among the flagellants?" Jason asked sleepily.

"You're thinking," she went on without answering, "that I'll never find a mate. Never go south, my father said. The world is a painted corpse; underneath the paint it has begun to decay. He tried to wake up his friends, but he only annoyed them. Soon they refused to see him. A little later my father brought my mother north and built this house with his own hands.

"Never go south, he told me. They are too soft there. They are dying. Stay here, he said. Some day a man will come to find you. And only the man who comes north freely will be worth having. That was before—" She stopped.

"Before what?" Jason muttered. He was very sleepy.

"I don't think you're too old," Diana said softly. "It's only," she said wistfully, "it's only that I think there should be something more."

Her words were buzzing in Jason's ears. He slept.

He dreamed....

Around him the world was dying. When he had started out it had seemed very beautiful. The foliage had been a brilliant green strewn with colorful flowers—yellow, scarlet, blue, every shade. But the whip in his hand rose and fell, and where it fell the world crumbled.

Trees turned to dust that floated slowly to the earth. Flowers wilted. It spread like contagion.

Soon he was walking in a gray desert, featureless and infinite. Gray dust rose in little clouds from his footsteps. It coated his body and face; it filled his nose, choking, dry. The whip in his hand rose and fell, pitiless, without end.

In the middle of the desert was a house. Perhaps he could get a drink here, something to wash down the dry death that choked him. He knocked at the door. There was no answer. He hammered. Only the echo of his pounding answered, and that was dull and muted. He raised his whip and lashed the door.

The door began to bleed. As it bled, it crumbled into gray dust. When it had crumbled away, he stepped through the doorway. He was back in the gray desert.

He began to cry. The tears dropped dustily, and then they too dried, and he could cry no more. He turned to look back. The false front was crumbling. It was sham, like the rest, and only led back to the desert.

"Jeri!" he shouted. "Jeri!"

But it was useless. He had whipped Jeri to death a long way back, before he had discovered that the world was dying.

The desert was featureless again. He was lost in it. He could never find his way out. *Which way is north?*

He began to walk. The whip in his hand rose and fell....

Eventually he saw it rising above the desert, a tall, silver spire pointing skyward, set in an oasis of green. He plodded toward it, through the gray dust. It grew nearer. He began to run. There was life, there was promise, there was the future.

He began to meet others in the desert.

They were sauntering, talking languidly. They were walking in the wrong direction. He grabbed their arms. He tried to tell them. They stared at him coldly until he let them go.

"A man must be free," they said, "to go any way he pleases."

They went on walking in the wrong direction.

A tub was sunk in the desert. A man was sitting in it, neck deep in water. Jason tried to pull him out, to drag him toward the spire.

"No, father," the man said. "Clare is waiting."

His head sank slowly beneath the surface of the water. Little bubbles came up and then ceased.

The spire was closer. There were more people now. Some came in pairs, one beating the other. They were bare to the waist, men and women. When Jason looked at their backs, however, he saw that they were only bones, only spines and ribs. When the whips fell, gray dust puffed out.

"There!" Jason said, pointing toward the spire. "There! Where are you going?"

They all pointed in one direction, where a gray mist stretched all across the horizon. Two by two, they disappeared into it.

And then there were those who passed with their faces hidden, singly. They too went toward the gray mist.

Jason went on toward the spire. The whip in his hand rose and fell. The back in front of his was soft and white and feminine, and the lashes cut into it cruelly, but the spire grew taller as they came close. He had to reach it soon or the desert would win.

"Faster!" he croaked.

He struck again and again. The flesh opened red mouths to kiss the lashes. "Faster!" he shouted. They were almost there.

The woman turned her head to look back over her shoulder at him. "I don't think you're too old," she said. "It's only that I think there should be something more."

But they were at the spire now. It towered above them hundreds of feet. It was a fountain, spraying life-giving water high into the air. Jason looked up expectantly, saw the drops glittering in the sun, waited for it to fall upon him, to wash him clean again.

They fell. They were not water but gray dust.

Jason watched the spire crumble away....

It was dawn when he woke up. The world was gray, but slowly it grew brighter and golden.

Jason lay still, enjoying a momentary feeling of peace. Then he turned his head. Diana lay across the room, against the opposite wall, on a pallet of skins. She was asleep. One white arm was thrown out along the floor. Her face was relaxed and young.

Suddenly Jason knew what was wrong. The room had not been lived in for a long time. There was only the simple cooking pot. There were no extra clothes, nothing to hunt with, and the handmade furniture was falling apart from disuse. Where had Diana lived?

Jason sat up and found he could move his back almost without pain. He put his legs over the edge of the bunk. Cautiously, he stood up. Dizziness swept over him, and he clutched the bunk until it passed. After a moment he felt better.

The whip was in the corner, near the bunk, where Diana must have tossed it. He walked to it quietly, picked it up. He tiptoed to the door. There, he turned and looked at Diana once more. What was she? What did she want? She stirred restlessly.

He pulled at the door. It came open with a small squeak. The morning air came in, fresh and cold. The flesh stirred on Jason's bare chest. He shivered. He looked back.

Diana's eyes were open.

"Where are you going?" she whispered.

"North."

"You can't," she said. She rose on one elbow. The far covering slipped down. She caught it to her breast. Her shoulders gleamed whitely. "They'll kill you."

"Not if I'm one of them. I've come a long way. I have to find out. I've troubled you enough."

"You weren't any trouble." She frowned. "You aren't one of them. They'll know. You're still alive."

Jason shrugged. Why doesn't she want me to go?

She looked away from him and back again. "Wait," she said.

He turned his back and waited. He heard rustlings behind him. "All right," she said. He turned. She was dressed, but only up to the waist. Her breasts were high and firm and young.

"I'm going with you."

"No."

"Yes," she said firmly. "How can you stop me?" She came toward him. He stepped back and she brushed past him and went outside. She turned her back to him. "Whip me," she said. It was like his dream.

"I can't," he said hoarsely.

She turned and took the whip. She swung it up and over her shoulder. The lashes bit in. She swung again. Blood welled in the shallow cuts. The third time he grabbed the lashes in his hand and jerked the whip away.

"No more," he said violently.

She raised her head. Tears glistened in her eyes. "Will you let me go?"

His voice shook. "If you promise never to do that again."

She looked at him steadily. "All right."

He started to say something but he changed his mind and set his jaw grimly. He handed her the whip and walked to where the path began. He heard her soft footsteps behind him. He headed north.

After a moment he said, "Go ahead." He waited.

"All who go north," she whispered, "do not have to be whipped."

"Use the whip," he said. He clenched his teeth. The whip swished through the air and coiled lightly around his shoulder.

"Harder!" he said.

She whimpered. He walked on waiting. The whip came down, biting in. Jason's back straightened. Diana gasped.

How do they stand it? Jason thought: *Hour after hour. Day after day.*

"Again," he said.

He walked on north. Diana followed, sobbing....

"Why don't you just tell him?"
"It wouldn't work. He must find out for himself."
"You know best, I suppose. I was born up here."
"You don't realize the strength of a system of beliefs. They must be broken gradually, one by one. He must come north because he wants to

break free, because he wants something he does not know exists. I have done my part. Now you must do yours."

"You're taking a lot of trouble for one man."

"We need him. We need his knowledge. We need his strength. But he will need help. You must be there to give it to him."

"I don't think I'm going to like him, Micah."

"For your sake, Diana, I hope you don't...."

At noon they stood side by side, tiredly, at the top of a long hill. Below them lay the ruins. Mile after mile it stretched, flattened rubble, with here and there a finger of metal or rock pointing toward the sky. It was as barren and desolate as the desert of Jason's dream. Nothing moved. Nothing lived. It was the ruins.

"Who built it?" Diana whispered. It wasn't necessary to whisper. They were all alone on the hill. But she whispered.

"Men," Jason said. "But what destroyed it? Time?"

They looked at the ruins for a long time.

"Why do they come here?" Jason said at last. "And where are they now?" Diana had folded her arms across her breasts for warmth. Now she pointed toward the ruins. "There!" she said. "There they are!"

Jason looked. Two small black dolls were walking stiffly, unreally, across the rubble. "They aren't afraid," Jason said.

He turned to Diana. "You don't have to come any farther."

"What do you mean?"

"I don't know why you took me in or why you came with me, but it wasn't for the reasons you gave. You never lived in that house."

"Yes, I did," she said. Tears gathered in her eyes. "Long ago. And you're wrong about my coming with you. I didn't have to do that. But I can't tell you anything more. You'll have to trust me."

"Why should I?"

She dropped her arms at her side and looked at the ground. "Don't you know?" she whispered.

He caught her shoulders and turned her toward him. He raised her head with one hand. He kissed her lips. Her arms went around him. When they parted, her hands were stained with red.

"Perhaps I do," he said.

Hand in hand they went down into the ruins.

They traveled across a neck of the ruins, picking their way carefully. Pits, some filled with rain water, and deadfalls were dangerous. By scrambling and running where they could, they managed to keep the figures in sight for a long time. When they lost them, the ruins were a mile behind.

They came upon a wide strip of unbroken stone. After a little way, it dipped down into a wide hole in the ground. Giant doors had once sealed the opening, but they had long since sagged from their fastenings.

For the first few minutes, the smooth, unnatural cave curved and twisted. As it grew darker, they found torches flickering against the wall. Then the road straightened and went down at a steeper angle.

Jason began to shiver. "The air—" he began.

"The torches still burn brightly," Diana said.

Jason took a deep breath and went on. A few steps later they heard it. It was a low moaning sound, like an underground river or a lost wind. It grew louder. The torches grew more frequent.

They broke into the cavern unexpectedly.

Backs faced them everywhere, bleeding, scarred, mutilated. Hundreds of them. Jason gasped and shuddered.

"Too many!" he muttered. "Too many! How do they stand it?"

Diana grasped his arm. After a moment he stopped shaking. The moaning had been coming from here. They were all moaning and swaying, facing a raised portion of the stone floor on the other side of the huge artificial cave. It was a vast lament which seemed to come unconsciously from deep inside them, like a mass keening for lost souls.

On the stone platform was a table of some kind, a crude wooden table. The table held a rusty metal sphere. Around it gleamed small lumps of silvery metal. Beside the sphere was a heavy hammer. Back against the wall was the familiar figure of the Prophet.

The end of the world. A premonition of disaster swept over Jason. He turned to Diana. "That's it!" he whispered. "That's the fuel-metal."

As they looked, a scarred figure came up on the platform and put down another lump of metal.

Someone brushed past Jason. Jason caught only a glimpse of the man's face before he disappeared in the crowd.

"Theron!" Jason shouted.

He pressed forward, squeezing himself between stolid backs. "Theron!"

Echoes bounced off the smooth walls. "THERON Theron theron."

The moaning began to lose its rhythm, to change. Jason ignored it. Fear was mounting in him. He pushed ahead. "Theron!"

A hand clutched at his shoulder and slipped away. Someone was following him, and the bodies in front of him were getting more unwieldy, harder to push apart.

"Jason!" someone said.

Something hit the back of his head.

He reeled forward, almost falling. "Theron," he moaned.

He was hit again.

"Jason!" The voice seemed very far away.

And then a third blow fell, and the cavern went dark as Jason felt himself falling, falling forever....

Jason turned his head, trying to get his breath. He opened his eyes. He was lying face down on a grassy slope. His head ached dully. He tried to move. His legs were tied together; his hands were fastened behind him.

Looking up the long hill, Jason could see nothing but the darkening sky and clouds that were turning gold in the long rays of the invisible sun. They dripped down the west like fleece. Infinitely desirable. Eternally unattainable.

Diana! Jason struggled against his bonds. Quivering pain shot down his back, but they were too strong, too tight. When he had succeeded in rolling over on his side, he stopped fighting and relaxed, satisfied. He watched the violet creep up the sky and remembered.

Thus we lie and watch darkness enshroud the world.

Diana had hit him. He had been hit from behind, and she had been behind him. When he was coming close to the secret, she had betrayed him. What did she want? What—or who was she trying to protect?

Something defied the night. The sun leaped back into the sky, a swirling ball of fire that hurt the eyes. The ground rocked beneath him. Heat blasted him. The sun swept up and up, dimming, fading in the dirty gray clouds that climbed with it and hesitated, spread, and climbed again, whiter, purer. Far up it spread out like a vast canopy.

The sun was gone now, gone for good. The darkness came quickly, a velvet backdrop for the cloud.

More rubble, Jason thought. And then, bitterly, *Purification!*

Jason knew the answers now, and it didn't matter. He knew where men came from and what they were and why they shunned the ruins. He knew why men went north.

We remember the ruins, he thought, *the ruins where the past is buried. But it is not buried deep enough. It is buried in us, too, and we remember how we destroyed ourselves. The memory is a sickness that infests us all. Some of us come north to die, scourging ourselves, and the rest choose other deaths at home, quiet, dusty deaths.*

There should be a word for it, he thought, *one word to wrap up the regret we feel for something we have done and the penance we inflict upon ourselves. One word for the emotion, no less real for being sub-conscious, and the punishment, no less severe for being misunder-stood. As I felt about Jeri.*

We destroyed the past, and now we have destroyed the future. We will never leave this place of fatal memories.

It didn't matter. The bonds were tight, and Diana was gone. The thought intruded, *But who carried me here?* It puzzled him. He would lie here, he decided, and think about it. He would have a long time to think before he got too weak.

Diana! he thought.

"Jason!" came the answer.

He smiled. Perhaps it would not be so long. Already his mind was beginning to trick him. "Diana!" he called.

"Jason!" The voice sounded close. "Jason." Something fumbled at his feet and then at his wrists. They were free. His mind was free for the first time, too. Little things began to fall into place. *All who go north do not have to be whipped.*

Jason turned, sat up. "I spoiled it, didn't I? You were trying to get the fuel-metal. When I lost my head, you abandoned the attempt to save me."

"No, no," she said. "You're wrong. You saved us. We didn't know it would do that." She gestured to the cloud that was slowly breaking up. "If we hadn't brought you out, we would have been there."

Jason nodded. The intent didn't matter. The intent never mattered, not to the results or the mind. "Where are the others?"

"North." Diana was quiet, crouched on her knees beside him, staring steadily at his face.

"Theron?"

"Theron and Micah and the others. Several hundred who decided that freedom is not as important as striving."

"But I am free?" She nodded. "And you?" he asked. She did not answer; her eyes did not waver.

He caught her hard and pulled her toward him. She came into his arms. He held her close.

Man had taken a wrong turn. He destroyed himself because he was afraid to live. He shunned the ruins except to seek death. He was afraid to learn the truth.

Where was the truth? It did not lie south. There was only the easy death. And the ship, the spire, would never be fueled, not in his life.

Where was the truth? It was wherever men sought it, eternally unsatisfied.

Jason felt free of an ancient burden. "Diana," he sighed.

In the morning they skirted the ruins and headed north. Somewhere they had lost the whip.

JACKPOT FOR JULIE

It all started with a dog.

The dog was a 3-1 favorite in the sixth at Las Vegas. She was a sweet, chestnut filly named June Bride, and she barely nosed an iceman's crowbait out of seventh.

There were only eight horses entered.

These are the times that try men's souls. Art Holliday turned from his long, incredulous inspection of the odds posted on the black tote board in the infield, unburdening himself of a great weight of disillusion.

The sudden awareness that a girl was watching him wiped the words away. Hastily she turned her gaze downward but not before he had caught a brief, enigmatic glint of speculation in soft brown eyes.

Slim, white fingers were methodically decimating a parimutuel ticket.

After disillusion, the realization that there is still beauty in the world has the impact of a five-inch shell. Wise women know this and make the most of it; they call it "catching a man on the rebound."

Art had recognized the phenomenon abstractly; now it became practical knowledge.

The girl's crisp, cool frock matched her eyes, and her cropped, feathered hair, which matched the frock, was the color of June Bride, the sweet, chestnut filly.

A gambler is suspicious of coincidence and unduly trustful of hunches. Art's hunch was that this filly would never run out of the money.

"You, too?" he said ruefully, fanning his worthless tickets.

His technique had never been so successful. Within five minutes, they were sharing a table in the clubhouse.

Her name was Julie Bliss.

She had stopped over in Las Vegas to win a thousand dollars, but it had begun to appear more difficult that it had seemed on the train.

Women have hunches, too, but they call it intuition. It is a notoriously poor, untrustworthy thing, and its reasons make the male mind reel.

Julie Bliss—June Bride. Who could miss the coincidence? Besides, this was June, and Julie would soon be a bride.

Art had already been hit by a five-inch shell. Beside this new blow, it was only a firecracker. To discover simultaneously that the chips are already down and that the Dealer is using a cold deck is a shock from which many men never recover.

Art was no welsher. He recognized the odds and played the game according to the rules, accepted his winnings as if he were used to it and paid his losses as if they were winnings. *Life is a gamble!* he reminded himself sternly.

"Why do you need a grand?" Art asked.

"For my wedding," said Julie.

To Art, weddings were a foreign track. Rumor had it that a simple ceremony was priced as low as a parimutuel ticket—although the risk involved was infinitely greater and the chances of picking a winner dishearteningly small. One grand, therefore, represented a startling price-spread.

"You don't understand," Julie said, shaking her head at the ignorance of men when it came to the warp-and-woof of existence. "I have my trousseau but there's the wedding dress to buy, the announcements, invitations, flowers—oodles of them for everyone—the reception, the caterer..." Her eyes withdrew into the distant, happy time.

That seemed like too fat a roll for every girl to put up, but Julie explained carefully that the bride's parents took care of it. But her parents were dead.

Some girls—for one reason or another—believe in long engagements. Julie was one of them. She wanted to be very, very sure that she was doing the right thing. She had gone as far from David as she could go without leaving the country; she had taken a job in Los Angeles as a secretary. For six months she had saved her money and studied the condition of her heart.

Now she was going home to be married—to one of those green, lakeside suburbs north of Evanston, Illinois—Wilmette, perhaps, or Winnetka—with her heart determined but her finances inadequate. She had saved one hundred dollars, and one thousand was the absolute minimum for respectability.

"People might pass that off as modest or discreet," she confided.

"How about Junior?"

Julie recoiled. People accustomed to wealth develop an ambivalent attitude toward money; it's not important unless you don't have it. "David wouldn't understand. As for his parents....!"

It sounded, Art thought, like a delightful family, and he could understand, all right, why Julie was hurrying home to marry into it. What he couldn't understand was why true love had to be a banker.

"In a town like that, starting married life is difficult at best. If you start off wrong, it's impossible. I know; I've lived there. But no one can look down their noses at a girl with one thousand dollars."

"Even if she won it at Las Vegas?" Art asked slyly.

That was different. The wealth of Wilmette (or Winnetka) was solid. It was based on realities: a distillation of Chicago beef and pork and grain and the steel rails that carried them. Beside it, other money melted like fairy gold at the touch of iron.

Gambling was not only considered dishonest in the lake-shore suburbs—far worse, it was disreputable. As a matter of fact, Julie felt that way about it herself.

"They don't need to know where it came from," she said, frowning until tapered eyebrows almost met.

"So you would take it—if you could get it."

She looked at him out of dark eyes suddenly wise and ancient. "Women have always known that sometimes they can't be particular. Otherwise the human race would have been extinct long ago. This is my chance. It's win or go back to L. A."

Art studied her objectively. "Gambling," he said soberly, "isn't so much a sport, you know, as a psychological device for asking Fate a vital question: Am I lucky or unlucky? And people have two reasons for gambling: to win or to lose."

"That's silly," Julie objected. "Who wants to lose?"

"There are some persons to whom it's psychologically important to get the answer: 'You are unlucky!' Or, on a more conscious plane, some persons want Fate to make the decision they can't make themselves."

Art's eyes were a little grim, a little pitying, and more than a little sympathetic as Julie explained that she realized her chances were only one in ten—but that was better than no chance at all.

He had to tell her the bad news. The odds weren't determined by the amount of money she had divided by the amount of money she hoped to win. At best, the odds were only one in a hundred.

Any gambler who accepted those odds should have his head shrunk.

Julie's first handicap was ignorance.

Everything she had heard about beginner's luck was paid advertising. For every tenderfoot who walked away with a few cartwheels jingling in his jeans, a thousand hit the trail considerably wiser and lighter.

On top of that was the vigorish. Even if she had average luck—which would let her break even if the house paid correct mathematical odds—the house percentage would soon eat up her capital.

"It's a thousand or nothing," Julie said firmly. "The hundred is worthless."

"Julie," Art said soberly, "you would get a better run for your money if you walked up to the first stranger and bet it would rain within the next hour—and in this part of Nevada it doesn't rain five inches a year."

Julie studied her glass, making little rings of moisture on the table top. "When a person really needs help," she said slowly, not looking up, "there's always someone who can give it to you, will want to—if you can only find him."

"What kind of help?"

"Someone who knows how to win."

Art was shaken at the thought. "There ain't no such person. If there were, there wouldn't be any casinos."

Julie looked up, letting Art feel the full impact of her eyes. "You! You know about gambling. Help me! Please."

Art struggled. "The only thing I know is how not to lose."

"How?"

"Don't bet!"

"But you know so much more than I do. Surely you could improve my chances—"

"Me?" Art let himself consider the proposition seriously. "Help you marry some stuffed heir from the lakeshore?"

"I'll be honest with you." Julie blushed prettily. "That's why I picked you up. You will, won't you? I know you will."

Art smiled recklessly. "Why not? But don't blame me if you lose the roll!" But he knew it was a sucker play. She would blame him; she couldn't help it. And if she won, she'd be off to Wilmette (or Winnetka). Art couldn't win.

"When do we start?" Julie asked eagerly.

She had the gambler's fever already.

"Not at the races for sure," Art said flatly. "Gamblers have a couple of old sayings: all horseplayers die broke, and never bet on anything that can't talk. Horses are bad bets. Parimutuel betting makes that as certain as taxes. It's just a way of letting the customers bet among themselves with the state government and the track taking a slice off the top before the winners collect."

"Then why do people bet on horses?"

"Horseplayers have been asking themselves that question since the Assyrians. The best reason is the one that man gave who was warned not to sit into a certain poker game—it was crooked. 'I know,' he said, 'but what can I do? It's the only game in town.'"

"Aren't there systems or something?"

"There's two drawbacks to all systems. One—they need a large starting capital. Two—they always go broke. Some system players double-up on favorites. At Gulfstream Park, Florida, twenty-one favorites in succession ran out of the money. Some bet on jockeys. One year Eric Guerin rode seventy-five consecutive losers.

"Sure, I know a man who gets a twenty percent return on his money. With him it's a job, and he has the patience to bet only the one race in twenty that can be handicapped successfully.

"You don't want twenty percent in a year. You want one thousand percent in—in—"

"Oh," she said innocently, "I'll have to have it tonight. My train leaves tomorrow morning."

Art was stunned. Luck wasn't a dog to be summoned. It needed a chance to sniff them out.

Julie was helpless.

The date of the wedding was set, and there were preparations which couldn't wait a day longer.

For a moment Art watched her with worshipful eyes as she stood up. Small, slim, lovely — she would make some man a wonderful — and unpredictable — wife.

Art sighed. It wouldn't be him.

Along Highway 91, outside the city limits of Las Vegas but not beyond the incandescence of Glitter Gulch, the greatest concentration of inert gas in the world, sprawls a fabulous collection of multimillion-dollar hotels known as the Strip. It is incorporated into two townships: Paradise A and Paradise B.

As fabulous as the hotels are their attractions: exquisite cuisines and priceless entertainment in delightful supper clubs. Approvingly, Art watched Julie attack a medium rare T-bone steak with rare appetite.

He approved even more because he knew that she was worried.

Julie belonged in that nebulous but unmistakable classification of humanity known as "nice girls." There is a line — though it may waver and bend — between the things that a girl may and may not accept from a comparative stranger. If it is a matter of type — gifts, say, like jewelry, perfume, of lingerie — the decision is obvious: no, thank you sir. But when the line must be drawn between qualities or quantities, a nice girl may often find herself in a quandary.

In itself, a meal is beyond reproach. But when a meal is exquisite and the entertainment is priceless — a girl must count the cost, and it was Julie's experience that for any expenditure over twenty dollars a man expects at least a small return.

Art waved a hand toward the entertainers and the orchestra. "You know what they are? Shills. The management loses money on this place—on the hotel itself. But it gets everything back—with interest—in the casino."

Julie looked up earnestly. "Why don't you give it up?"

Art bit his lip to keep from smiling. "All this, you mean? This sordid occupation? The dismal surroundings?"

"You don't belong here," she said, studying his face. "How did you get mixed up in it?"

"The story of my life, eh? My downfall? My degradation? I'll tell you," he said, straight-faced. "It started with my birth. I was born here, and that's how it began. I was doomed by my environment. Oh, I had a normal boyhood—slipping my allowance into the neighborhood slot machine when nobody was looking. A Reno gambling house gave me a scholarship to college. I wasn't the only one, of course, but I accepted it. I suppose I allowed myself to be bought by the gambling interests, and my moral fiber began to disintegrate—"

Julie's cheeks got red. "You're teasing me. You needn't go on. I can't stand the awful details. You became a gambler."

"In a sense I never was anything else. Who is?"

"Why don't you get an honest job? This kind of money is fairy gold. It can never buy anything worthwhile. You've got a college education—"

"Hold on there," Art drawled. "As I understand it, you want a little of that there gold in these hyar hills."

"That's different."

"It always is."

By no accident, the gaming room was adjacent to the supper club. The floor plan of the Strip hotels is ingeniously contrived so that the facilities for trying a person's luck are never far away. The opportunity is enough; the hotels are making expenses.

Art vetoed the slots. Theoretically, the bandits returned as much as any game in the casino, including craps. Practically, it was impossible to win any large amount. The limit was too low.

They threaded their way through the well-dressed players standing for a moment or making their way from game to game. They passed green-felted tables and their mesmerized circles of devotees: craps, keno, roulette, faro, blackjack, poker, chuck-a-luck....

The experienced gambler picks a game in which the vigorish is low, craps, mostly, where the house percentage is only two percent, compared with three for faro, five for roulette, seven for chuck-a-luck, and up.

"But isn't dice just luck?" Julie objected.

"Outside of knowing the odds, the only legal skill is knowing when to stop. We know that already: one grand."

Julie took a deep, shaky breath. "Isn't there something that isn't so risky?"

"In some games skill is more important. Poker, say."

"Are you a good poker player?"

"Fair."

"Then let's try that," she decided nervously. Already her cheeks were flushed with excitement and her voice quivered.

"Stay here," Art said, moving away. "It's not every game you can win a grand. I'll ask the pit boss." He paused and smiled at her encouragingly. "Sit behind me. With your luck—and my skill—maybe we've got a chance."

Out of darkness and chaos, the overhead light carved a cone of life, brilliant, almost tangible. Beneath it was an octagonal, felt-topped table. Smoke wavered upward, striated, thick. The fans worried the smoke and then sucked it away.

It was one a.m. In front of Art were neat stacks of chips and silver dollars. He had not counted them—it is unlucky to count—but he knew how much it was within a few dollars: $500. Julie, sitting behind him with fevered eyes, had refused to quit.

His eyes shaded by an immemorial green eyeshade, the dealer deftly scaled cards to the six players. Art collected them, one by one, slid them together, picked them up, squeezed them apart: *Ace — five — ace — ace — seven.*

The first player passed. The next, a bald, bullet-headed Westerner in a red string tie and a white shirt stained with crescents of sweat, opened the pot for $10. Three men stayed.

"Bump it twenty," said Art.

The first man tossed away his cards. "Up thirty," said the opener in a surprising tenor voice.

One of the three callers, caught between the raisers, dropped out. "And fifty," Art said.

That was the last raise. The opener called, and one of the other two.

The opener took one card. The second player drew three. Art hesitated and called for two cards.

He squeezed the cards apart again: *Ace — ace — eight — ace — queen.* He hadn't helped.

The opener studied his hand expressionlessly, glanced at the pot, and looked at Art's stacks of chips as if he were counting them. He began leveling off piles of blue chips in front of him. "Three hundred and ninety," he said, pushing them into the center of the table.

Art leaned back in his chair as the intervening player dropped hastily. "Can he do that?" Julie whispered anxiously.

"Pot limit," Art muttered. "He's within his rights. The question is: do we call or fold? If we lose it'll wipe us out. If we win, we've—"

"Let's play poker," growled the opener.

Art straightened up. "It's the little lady's money," he said evenly. "She deserves a say." He leaned back to Julie. "If we win, we've got your thousand and then some."

"Have we got the best hand?"

Art shrugged helplessly. "I can't read him. We had the best hand going in. He opened with two pair. His bet says he filled up—if he isn't bluffing. He's got'em or he hasn't. We lose or we win. Understand?"

Julie shook her head in bewilderment. "You mean it's a fifty-fifty chance?"

"Maybe a little better. The chances of improving two pair are about one in eleven. Also, he's bluffed before...."

Julie looked down at the stack of chips in front of Art and then at those mounded in the center of the table. "Call!"

Art counted out the chips. It took all but a lonely cartwheel.

Slowly the opener laid down his hand: two kings, then three fours.

Art sighed heavily and tosses in his hand face up and turned quickly to Julie, picking up the silver dollar. "Sorry, kitten," he said penitently, "if I'd been smarter...."

Her white face stopped him. "That's all right," she said. Her voice was almost steady. "Instead of one chance in ten or one chance in a hundred, you gave me better than one in two."

Art held out the dollar on his fingertips. Julie bent his fingers over it. "Keep it—as a souvenir."

"What are you going to do?"

"Go back to L.A."

Art caught a slim hand and led her away from the table. "Look! I don't know what kind of tinhorn you're engaged to—I don't want to know—but if he doesn't want you with just one silver dollar"—he tossed it, glittering into the air and caught it deftly with one hand—"then he doesn't deserve you at all."

Julie shook her head unhappily. "It's not him; it's me. I can't face it unless I can do it right."

"Are you sure you love this fourflusher?"

Julie's head came up proudly. "Of course I'm sure!"

"It's a funny kind of love," Art said slowly, "that lets chance flip the coin on your marriage."

Julie's face was turned away. Art studied her profile: the straight sweep of forehead, the precise little nose—pinched a little now at the nostrils—the soft parentheses of lips holding between them a thousand things unsaid.... They trembled now; white teeth bit down to hold them still.

Love! Art thought despairingly. *I know what love is.*

"Wait here," he said. "I've got an idea."

Floor managers—known less formally as pit bosses—listen politely; it's part of their job to assure the customer that his money is as good as anybody's. This one, in tuxedo and starched white front, listened to Art with something more than ordinary courtesy. His professional smile slowly faded into interest.

"That's a chunk of dough," he muttered.

There was no doubt about that. "Look what you're buying," Art pointed out. It's no secret that established operators love to see patrons win; on occasion, they even murmur a silent prayer. There isn't any better advertising.

In 1950 a young man made twenty-eight successive passes; the Desert Inn enshrined the dice, and the story was circulated nationwide. Not long afterwards two system players took a couple of Reno roulette wheels for several grand. It was a running story for days from Vancouver to Key West, and the owners begged the gamblers to stop before they lost it all back.

"No crooked stuff," the pit boss warned. "That's out."

"I'm crying," Art said scornfully.

"So it should get out—so you're a philanthropist. When it's raining money, the least you can do is hold out your hat. All you have to do is look the other way."

"You're faded! There's an unused table in the back. I'll meet you there in five minutes."

"With the busters," Art added firmly.

The pit boss hesitated and nodded.

It was a long, green-topped table subdivided by white lines and railed in green, translucent plastic. At first they were alone at the table—Art, Julie, and the pit boss—but word spread swiftly in the psychic way peculiar to gambling—and within minutes a three-deep crowd was pressing curiously around the table. A few tried to get down their bets, but the pit boss shook his head at them firmly. "Private game!"

"I don't want to throw them," Julie said. "I don't even know the rules."

"Never mind," said Art. "Just toss'em and pray. This gentleman knows your problem, and he's offered a chance for you to win what you need. We'll bet your silver dollar and let it ride. Make ten straight passes and you've won $1,024. Okay?"

Julie nodded dazedly. The transparent red cubes tumbled clumsily over the green and rebounded from the railing. A five and a four—nine. She came right back with a six and a three.

She had two silver dollars.

The next point required three tosses; then she had four cartwheels. After the third one she had eight, then sixteen, then thirty-two.

It was the beginning of myth. The table was enveloped in a charged silence like that before the lightning hits. Julie tossed out the dice without understanding anything except the growing mountain of silver dollars. Twice she rolled eleven, but otherwise she made it by point. Not once did she throw craps. Not once did she throw a seven.

After the eighth pass she had $256. After the next one, $512. On the tenth the mounded cartwheels had pushed themselves into a silver peak on the green meadow. The dice rolled past it and rebounded. A one and a three. Four.

The kibitzers groaned sympathetically. "Little Joe," Art whispered, staring down at the white spots.

"What's the matter?" Julie asked, looking up blankly, afraid suddenly that the mountain had melted away.

"Nothing," said Art, patting her arm. "Tough point, but you'll make it. Just keep rolling."

Julie's arm was tired. She rubbed it for a moment and then bounced the dice off the rail. They rebounded and spun crazily. One toppled: a three. The other turned, rolled: a one. Four. Her point.

Julie reached for the dice, but Art's hand closed over hers. "That's all. That's you thousand and twenty-four to boot. Time to quit."

Out of the crowd came a hoarse voice saying, "Don't be a sucker, lady. You're hot tonight. You got the touch. A few more passes and you'll break the bank!"

Julie's eyes unglazed. She shook her head. "That's enough."

In his office, the pit boss opened a check book on the wide, polished desk. "Name?"

Julie was studying the dice in her hand. "Julie Bliss."

"Address?"

She gave a Los Angeles street number.

"What's the groom's name and address?"

Behind Julie, Art shook his head warningly, but the pit boss only stared at him with puzzled eyes.

"David—" Julie began and broke off. "What do you need that for?"

"Interesting story," the manager said frankly.

"Tender, romantic, human interest stuff. 'Girl on way home to be married stops over in Las Vegas to win wedding expenses and makes ten straight passes to build one dollar into the thousand she needs.' The papers will eat it up."

"You can't put that in the papers!" Julie said quickly.

The manager was standing. "What do you mean?"

"And what's the matter with these dice?" Julie asked, turning to Art. "All the numbers are duplicated on the opposite sides. One has two ones, two fives, and two sixes. The other has two threes, two fours, and two fives."

The manager forced a smile and spread his hands helplessly. "You win, Miss Bliss. I'm fixed. I recognize it. Take the check—you've earned it." He ripped it free.

Julie looked down at the slip of paper as if it had hidden fangs. "There's something funny about all this. I don't think I won that honestly. That's why these dice are all wrong." She studied them again. "They can't make a seven!"

"Or two or three or twelve," Art said wearily.

"Why, I couldn't lose!" Julie exclaimed angrily. "No, thank you! I don't want your money! You can't buy a news story with that. David would never forgive me."

"Fine," the manager agreed instantly. "We'll all forget it." Slowly, carefully, he tore the check into shreds.

Dismally, Art watched them flutter into the wastebasket.

"How could you have done this to me?" Julie demanded angrily.

"I was just trying to help," Art shouted above her. People passing turned to look back into the corner of the casino where the two young people had stopped. "You wanted a thousand bucks. I was trying to get you a thousand bucks. If I'd had it I'd have given it to you. It's as simple as that."

"I would no more take your money," the girl said, her chin high, "than I would his."

"Okay!" Art thundered. "Be unhappy! Ruin your life because you need one grand and you're particular how you get it. It won't make me sad if your suburban Romeo has to wait ten years for you to save the scratch. I hope he gets tired of waiting."

"And I hope you have seven years bad luck!" Julie shouted, standing close, looking up fiercely into his face. "You and your horrible gambling dens!"

"They weren't so awful when you wanted some of their dirty money!"

"Ohhhh!" she groaned in helpless fury and turned away. "I hope I never see you again."

At the lonely desk in the lobby, Art finished printing his message on a pad of telegram blanks and swung toward the clerk, a harried young man with a blond, balding head. Someone bumped Art and tried to sneak ahead.

"I was here first," Art growled.

"Oh, no you weren't!"

"Julie!" Art exclaimed happily and then, glumly, remembering, "What are you doing here?"

"The same to you." Her voice had icicles hanging from it.

"I'm not laying off any bets," Art said, stiffening. "I know why you're wiring. You've weakened, haven't you? You're wiring Junior that he'll have to foot the wedding bills!"

"I am not!"

"Let me see!" Art challenged.

The clerk's head swiveled back and forth between them, helplessly. "I say," he tried several times—and gave up.

"A trade," she said.

Art drew back, clutching his message firmly. "Absolutely not."

"What are you afraid of?" Julie taunted.

Art breathed deeply, raggedly. "All right," he agreed suddenly. "Here!"

Their eyes flashed over the printing. Simultaneously they looked up. Simultaneously they said, "But this—"

"You're calling it off—for good," Art said, his eyes huge. "I should have known—I did know, only I wouldn't let myself believe it. You stopped here—to do something you disapproved of—because you wanted to lose. You wanted Fate to tell you not to marry Junior. You couldn't accept it as a conscious decision but...."

"You're asking someone in Lawrence, Kansas," she said in a low, puzzled voice. "The—"

"Bursar," Art supplied.

"For a thousand dollars!"

"Advance on salary. There's not much chance."

"You were going to give it to me," Julie accused. "Somehow you were going to make me accept it." Art looked down at his shoes. "You're the most confusing man. Sometimes you're one thing, the next minute, another. You talk like a gambler—but you're not—you've got a job somewhere—and then you talk like a—like a—"

"Psychology professor?" Art asked. He sighed. "That's what I am. Real romantic, isn't it. I'm here doing research for my doctoral thesis—'The Psychodynamics of Gambling.'"

"You were right about why I stopped in Las Vegas," Julie admitted, her eyes downcast like his. "I wasn't in love with David, but I wouldn't admit it to myself." She stood close to him, waiting. Her eyes flashed up. "A psychology professor indeed! You don't know much about women!"

Art knew enough.

Five minutes later the clerk tapped Art on the shoulder. "Are either one of you going to send a telegram?"

Art lifted his head. "Eh?" he said, his voice bemused. "Oh, sure. Send this one."

It was the telegram addressed to Wilmette (or Winnetka).

He tore up the other one. "I know where we can get the same thing for two bucks. Eh, Julie?"

She leaned back and looked at him critically. "If your theory is right, Professor Holliday, I came to Las Vegas to lose—but I've got a hunch I hit the jackpot."

THE MAN WITH ONE TALENT

Call me impresario.

Music is my business. It's a funny business, full of heart-break, full of laughter, and sometimes touched with magic. Like the time a boy with too much talent met a girl with too much money.

Luck handed me the talent where four dirt roads made a wide place for a country store and a gasoline pump. I one-fingered the Cadillac over a thin scattering of gravel to the pump and nudged the power brakes.

The Caddy was Ellen's, but the yokels thought it was mine, and I didn't straighten them out. Let them eye the long lavender sides with the continental grill on one end and the fishtails on the other—and the middle-aged man at the wheel who could afford it and the girl....

Ellen was asleep, huddled against the far door. She had stopped crying around about Terre Haute. If we were lost in the Ozark hills of Missouri, it was Ellen's fault—I never could read a map.

Ellen's fault, too, that we were halfway between Manhattan and Reno. I can't forget the look on her face as she realized that Nick hadn't loved her either. She had just driven in from Connecticut, where Nick wouldn't go, and she stopped in the doorway of the Manhattan apartment, her smile frozen on her face at the party noise and the girl who was with Nick. "Get me out of here, Sol," she said. "Quick."

But no one could carry a grudge against Ellen except the men she married. Not Ellen, soft-hearted, easy-to-deceive, little, sinned-against Ellen, plainer than usual with her reddened eyes and pale face. Poor, little rich girl. No talent, no judgment, no love. Just ten million dollars and the things it attracts.

Reno, I thought, here we go again.

A man with shoulders like a fullback before the pads are removed was stacking hundred-pound sacks of feed on the covered porch like they were foam-rubber pillows. I honked at him. Ellen stirred.

He came over, smiling openly, a boy, really, with dark, regular features, innocent eyes, and black, curly, untrimmed hair spilling over his forehead—a misplaced pagan god.

"Fill 'er up," I said.

It was an old-fashioned pump like I hadn't seen in ten years with a glass bowl that you had to pump the gas up into. I watched it drain down to beat the favorite game of these parts: stick the slicker. The boy was honest, and I gave him a five and told him to keep it.

He grinned like he wanted to say something but couldn't.

"Any place around here to get a decent meal?" I asked.

He shook his head, and just as I had him pegged as a dummy, he whispered, "You can get a sandwich inside."

I glanced skeptically at Ellen. Her eyes were open, pale blue and clear. They stared at the boy bending over to peer into the car, as I said quickly, "I guess—"

"We'll stop," Ellen finished softly.

It was late afternoon. The store was dark and the air was heavy with the smell of pickles and sawdust, feed, cloth, motor oil, spices....

By the meat counter was a rickety table covered with flour-sack gingham. We ordered cheese sandwiches from a white-whiskered old man with red eyes, because there isn't much anyone can do to a cheese sandwich.

I was hungry enough to eat mine, but Ellen only nibbled. As I finished, the air began vibrating. The meat counter's glass front rattled. *Earthquake!* I thought, as I sprang up, choking on the last bit of dry cheese.

They'd never forget it in the City if Sol Heron met his end in the hillbilly store....

"Luke!" said Whiskers, sharply.

The humming ceased. The glass stopped shaking. I hastily left a buck on the table and hustled Ellen toward the door.

The young giant intercepted us. "You from New York?" he whispered.

"There and elsewhere," I admitted, since he'd spotted the license. "Something wrong with your throat?"

He nodded. "How long," he whispered, "could a man live in New York on—say—fifty dollars?"

"Three-four days," I said, "if he can get there free and he don't eat."

The boy took it hard. I reached up to pat his shoulder. "Save your money, boy. Buy a farm."

"Can't." Beside me, the narrow, store window shivered noisily. A marvelously deep, vibrant voice. Instantly he dropped back to a whisper. "Got to get to New York. Got to."

"Forget it! Come on, Ellen."

Ellen held back. She turned to the boy, her sorrow seeking his. "Why?" she asked.

"Got to sing," he whispered, his eyes big and distant.

Ellen held out her left hand to me. "Five dollars, Sol." Ellen never has any money. I handed her the five. She handed it to the boy; it was a habit she couldn't break—giving money to men. "Mr. Heron's right," she said. "It's a bitter road. Stay home. Get married. Sing to your kids."

He stood, unmoving, staring at the crumpled bill in his hand, and I guessed it was more than he could save in six months. As we turned away, I thought: *Ellen got out cheap.*

Then I heard the most beautiful sounds I've ever known. It was *O Paradiso,* the tenor aria from *L'Africana,* but like no one had ever sung it before, exquisitely perfect.

Surprise paralyzed us; beauty held us tight until the middle of the aria when the boy's voice swelled with the vibrance of Vasco da Gama's emotion—and Paradise shattered.

The bowl on the gasoline pump cracked, let loose a red, aromatic cascade. The narrow store windows splintered. From inside came a hundred crashes. The boy stopped in mid-note, stricken.

"Luke!" came a scream from the store.

I glanced into the store. There wasn't a whole piece of glass. Pickles swam in the sawdust; baked beans dripped from the shelves; the meat in the counter glittered with a dusting of glass....

"Luke," the old man shouted, his whiskers looking even whiter against the red anger of his face, "yer fired!"

"Luke," I said impulsively, "you're hired."

I wheeled the Caddy around and we headed back east. "Who cares about Reno?" Ellen asked. "Let Nick go. He'll go," she added grimly. "I'll see to that."

What there was to learn about Luke, we learned. We learned that a man could live twenty-four years and have practically nothing happen to him.

Except the voice. That happened to him, and it was everything. The voice: every composer, dreaming his opera, hears it. The voice: the ancient Hebrews must have been hearing it when they wrote about the singing of angels. The voice—well, there are no words for perfection.

Through Missouri, he sang *Aida,* through Illinois, *Carmen* and *Les Huguenots.* In Indiana, he gave us *L'Elisir d'Amore* and *Pagliacci,* in Ohio, *Rigoletto* and *Samson and Delilah,* in Pennsylvania, *La Bohéeme....*

French and Italian opera. They were good enough for Caruso; they were good enough for Luke. But that wouldn't always be true. Already, without stepping out on a stage, Luke was greater than Caruso.

Technically perfect, physically incredible—that was Luke. His range made baritone parts as accessible as the tenor ones. His pitch was infallible, his throat open, his tongue free, his breathing imperceptible, his voice warm and rich and expressive, his enunciation distinct. And the resonance....!

Singing reached its peak in the *bel canto* of 18th Century Italy. After that singers never worked as hard. Wagner increased the power of the orchestra, and sonority became more important than purity and expressive phrasing....

For a number of reasons, there had been nothing to compare with Luke since the legendary Farinelli.

And Luke came out of the Ozark hills. Fantastic? True, but the same forces that fashioned the *bel canto* shaped Luke's superb natural gifts: relentless training.

Luke's mother was Italian, her father a noted tenor. His voice failed in his sixties, and he went to live with the daughter in America and the big, rough American soldier who had taken her away. Giuseppe met Luke and heard his voice and wept. From that day, he lived for Luke's voice.

Like Caffarelli in the 18th Century, Luke was kept to one sheet of exercises for five years. And he developed his voice against the Ozark's wooded hills until it filled the valleys with incomparable sound.

He learned how to breathe silently and how to control the breath so that Lablache might have said of him as he said of

Rubini, "Although I sang a duet with him I could not discern *when* or *how* he breathed."

Luke learned how to keep his throat open and his tongue free, how to draw out his notes and to do it so quietly that the least breath produced a note that would swell to the most sonorous and then die away.

When Luke was nineteen his parents died of one of those nameless backwoods diseases. A year later his grandfather followed them to the little family graveyard far from Italy and La Scala.

Before he died, Giuseppe said, "Go to New York, Lucas. Go to the Metropolitan. I have done for you all I can. Sing for the maestro. He will know that you are the great singer, greater than Caruso, greater than Rubini... But now—sing just for me...."

The evil days came, the years when he was all alone with his voice. The hilltop farm, where he had pushed the plow through the stubborn soil and boomed his voice against the hills, would never earn enough, and he couldn't sell it. He needed the money; it took a lot of money to get to New York, and money was hard to get. Especially for Luke.

He was big and strong, and he liked work, but as his reputation spread across the hills, jobs became hard to keep and harder to find. Inevitably, no matter how sincerely he promised, he broke into song, and the song broke up his job.

It was no use leaving the hills—the closer to civilization, the worse his predicament. Because of his voice. It was too good.

I've know people like that before; I've heard of more: great actors, great painters, great composers—men with one talent which is not so much a blessing as a tragedy, who are more possessed than possessing....

There had been no women in Luke's life. Earlier there had been no room for anything except singing. Later, they were afraid. A talent like Luke's has something satanic about it, a jealous something that owned him, against which no woman could compete.

Luke had to sing. Had to. And every time he sang, he destroyed.

You've heard how Caruso used to break wineglasses with the vibrations of his voice. Well, Luke did it with any kind of glass. Nothing made of shatterable glass within a radius of three hundred feet was immune.

That's why Luke couldn't keep a job. And nothing could keep him silent.

He sang to us through Missouri, Illinois, Indiana, Pennsylvania, and New Jersey. As Giuseppe had told him, we were going to New York. Going to the Met.—Luke Carpenter, who had a voice, Ellen McClure, who had a soft heart and ten millions dollars, and me, Sol Heron, who had a hard head and an unconquerable yen for the big time.

This time I'd hit it. Call me *impresario*, but I'm just a promoter like in the fight game, matching a boy in the preliminaries, bringing him along against the fighters he can beat, the fighters who can teach him something—But Luke didn't need that. He was ready now.

He had the voice. He had the repertoire. He could step out on the stage of the Met tomorrow night as Rudolpho in *La Boheme* and shatter the brittle complacence of the Manhattanites....

On top of that was the glass-business. I stared out the frosty windshield—safety glass doesn't shatter—at the Pennsylvania sugar maples wheeling by in their flaming autumn colors, and I thought: *A smart promoter can do it with nothing. I've got everything, the voice and the gimmick. No swoons, no screams. Just headlines. We can reach the top overnight.*

Maybe that's the way it would have been, maybe not. Ellen turned to me one evening and said, "We're playing it straight, Sol. No tricks. This is one thing that isn't going to be hoked up."

Her eyes were kind of dreamy-burning like Joan of Arc must have looked when the angel of the Lord gave her the word.

But we got the headlines anyway.

I picked up a paper first thing we reached the city, and it was on the front page:

SMASHER STRIKES AGAIN
Strange Phenomenon Heads East

....The trail of the lonesome panes, conservatively estimated at 50,000, leads through Missouri, Illinois, Indiana, Ohio, and Pennsylvania, following U.S. 40 east of St. Louis....

What came out of a clear sky to shatter 50,000 windows?

.... expansion and contraction, say some physicists. *Crystallization,* say others. *Inexplicable meteorological phenomenon,* say weathermen.

Poltergeists, people are whispering in the back country.

Mischievous boy with BB gun, say state patrolmen.

And 50,000 BBs, officers?

All we can say is: *Look out, New York!*

Luke's voice, my experiences, and Ellen's cash made a combination nothing could resist. Ellen explained carefully that Luke wasn't to know about the money. This time she was going to play it smart.

Sure, she was in love with the boy. Everybody could see that except Luke. Ellen wasn't going to tell him; she wasn't going to let herself get hurt again. As long as they weren't married, everything she did was uncompelled.

No precautions were necessary. Luke was in New York. He didn't know what money was or who had it or what it was good for.

We rented Carnegie Hall. There was a cocktail party beforehand, as usual. Ellen tried to veto it, but I held out, as I had for the minimum ad: *The Greatest Tenor Since Caruso*. But maybe Ellen was right.

Everything was going well—by which I mean everyone had a drink in his hand and was not acting too bored—when Ellen brought Luke into the room. He was something to see, even in the rented tuxedo we'd searched all Manhattan to find. She led him up to *the* critic, and introduced him.

"Hello," said Luke.

Suddenly everyone had a wet vest. Martini drinkers were holding only stems; those with highballs had a fistful of ice. One breathless girl who was only half of her cocktail dress to begin with did an impromptu hula as her Scotch-on-the-rocks disappeared into the obvious place.

The critic frowned at his wet hand, turned wordlessly, and stalked out of the room.

We should have been warned.

Luke was unaffected. We watched from the wings, Ellen and I, as he walked gracefully onto the stage looking poised and confident, no more like an Ozark hillbilly than Tagliavini or Björling, but I held Ellen's hands to warm them and to keep mine from trembling.

With a natural stage presence, Luke bowed to the polite applause and stood easily, waiting for the accompanist to begin.

We hit them hard right off, making sure to get the critics before their deadlines. Luke opened with *Che Gelida Manina* from *La Bohéme*. It starts softly, builds to a crescendo, and dies away. Luke opened his mouth and his throat and his heart. From the first note, the audience was his.

But as his voice swelled, I heard a warning ping from a baby spot beside us. And when Luke let out his voice in Rudolpho's introduction to Mimi—it happened.

First went the chandeliers, lovely things, tinkling, shattering, falling in a brittle rain. The lights exploded. The windows cracked open.

More than half of this over-thirty audience wore glasses. They broke on their faces.

Nothing could drown the magnificence of Luke's voice, not the background violence of the impermanent glass or the wild stampede of the audience out of the darkening hall. Luke didn't miss a note.

His voice died away for only a handful of people in the audience. And to them, in the darkness, he sang. To them, to those who stayed or were weak with beauty, it was the most wonderful thing that ever happened. He gave them: *Parmi Veder Le Lagrime* from *Rigoletto. Recitar* from *Pagliacci. Una Furtiva Vagrima* from *L'Elisir d'Amore. Lamento di Federico* from *L'Arlesiana....* He gave them beauty, pure, unalloyed.

I had the candles ready. He finished to their light, the small flames wavering in the chill wind pouring through the empty windows and sparkling from the powdered glass and splintered shards lying like snow and ice upon the floor and chairs. The audience didn't applaud. They were stunned.

The critics raved. "Greatest!" they wrote. "Finer than Caruso! An exquisite, unforgettable experience. Where has this young man been hiding himself?"

They said, also: "It is unfortunate that the recital was marred by ugly promotional trickery."

Ugly promotional trickery? Me? That hurt. "Now!" I said to Ellen. "We've got to hit 'em now before it's too late!"

Ellen glanced sideways at Luke, who was staring peacefully out the hotel window across the mountaintops of Manhattan. "No. It's his voice we're selling, not tricks. We play it straight."

So I played it straight, and what did it get us?

Surprisingly enough, it got us an audition at the Met. Among the few who had stuck out Luke's recital was the Met scout, and we got the big chance in spite of the shambles. The Carnegie Hall management was puzzled, but they couldn't pin the wreckage on us. And so far no one had connected our recent arrival with the 50,000 broken windows between Manhattan and the Ozarks.

I didn't know whether to be glad or sorry. Those 50,000 windows haunted me. On one hand, they were the solution to my promotional problems. On the other hand, they were, at a minimum price of two bucks apiece, a damage bill of one hundred thousand.

So we auditioned. Luke stood where Giuseppe had wanted him, on the golden stage, and there was a magic to it, naked as it was, and Luke sang. I can still hear it ringing—the acoustics not so good because the house was empty—and I can hear the chandeliers shattering, the floodlights crashing, and the Diamond Horseshoe exploding like a string of firecrackers.

Luke finished in darkness again. Someone brought in a candle. I looked at the Director's reverent face, and I thought: *maybe....*

But it was no use. The Director knew magic, but he knew, too, when magic was impossible. "Magnificent!" he said, "but how can we present an opera in darkness?"

He was crying as we left.

I could have told him about safety glass, but that was impractical, too. I kept thinking about the eye glasses and jewelry and damage suits and 50,000 windows.

"What now?" Ellen asked. Her voice was a little frightened, as if she could see Luke slipping away.

"There's one card left," I said. I played it.

The recording studios tried hard. The officers and sound men and technicians, they listened to Luke by candlelight in their sound-proofed studios, and all it cost them was their lights and some frosted control-room windows and five microphones.

They couldn't wax his voice. Microphones are more fragile than glass.

On the street outside, Luke looked frightened, too. "There is no place I can sing?" he asked. Glass shuddered nearby.

I took a deep breath and nodded. We had played it straight, Ellen and I. To save something incomparable from becoming spectacle and self-destruction, we had condemned it to silence.

And Ellen was afraid she had condemned herself, too. These last few days had changed her, I thought. She looked different, alive, clear-skinned, young. Well, she wasn't any older than Luke, really; money had aged her.

"Let's take a ride," I said.

We got out of the Caddy and rode until we reached Ellen's place in Connecticut, 1500 open acres of it. I drove the Caddy out on a hill and stopped it. We got out and sat on the grass, still green.

"Funny thing about a lot of money, a lot of talent," I said softly. "They aren't practical. Unless you can use them right, they only make you unhappy. Money isn't bad, and Art isn't bad, but they exist for themselves, not life. The more there is of them, the less of life."

Ellen looked thoughtful. "Luke's got too much talent, you mean. Too much for our kind of world, that's brittle, that breaks apart easily."

Luke nodded slowly. "Yes." Out here the word sounded right.

"In a more primitive society, there wouldn't have been that problem," Ellen said. "I guess we've all got some talent. The big difficulty is discovering it. If there's a royal road to happiness, it's finding your talent and being able to use it."

"What's yours?" Luke asked.

I guess he really noticed her for the first time.

"I don't know," Ellen said. "I haven't found it yet. Maybe that's why I've never been happy. My grandfather was happy. He had a talent for making money—he made almost twenty million dollars before he died."

"That's a lot of money, I guess," Luke said.

Ellen shrugged. "Father's talent was spending it. He managed to be quite happy before he died, but he couldn't spend it all, not the way grandfather had it put away. I've got a little left."

A little. I whistled softly.

"But it's only trouble, like Sol said," Ellen went on, "unless you use it right. Luke, I think I've found a way to use it. I love you, Luke. Will you let me help you find out how to use your talent?"

I walked away from there, not fast, not slow. Nobody noticed. It was no place for a promoter.

That's it. Like I say, a funny business, full of heart-break, full of laughter, and sometimes touched with magic. Ellen's place.

Fifteen hundred acres without a window or anything else made of glass. Luke can sing without a worry in the world.

He sings to Ellen. He sings to an audience once in a while that gets invited up to a natural amphitheater tucked away among the hills. And he sings to a bunch of the most talented kids you'll find anywhere—he's teaching them, but not quite as good as he can because when the talent gets too big, he says, it starts eating up the man.

In a few years I can start my own opera house.

Ellen's found her talent: it's for loving.

And she's found a good use for her money. She paid for the damages to the Met and to Carnegie Hall and to 50,000 windows between Manhattan and Missouri. But most of all she paid for the development of a microphone that Luke's voice won't shatter.

Some records are being made that are the most fabulous things you ever heard. In a few months they'll be on the market, but I'm warning you, like the label says in big, red letters: WARNING—DO NOT PLAY THIS RECORD ON A HIGH-FIDELITY PHONOGRAPH.

That is—if you live in a glass house like most of us.

Sure, they could have distorted the recordings, but Luke said no. He said Giuseppe wouldn't have liked it.

So anybody who wants to hear the most magnificent voice in the world, ever, will have to do as I did—build a glass-free music room.

Expensive? For a couple of bucks you can buy half an hour of pure magic.

THE BIG ONE

The overhand right caught me coming in. Johnny was a sucker for throwing it. I was a bigger one for letting it catch me. In the brief moment between, I knew how old I was.

I saw the punch all the way, the glove getting bigger like a brown balloon, but I just couldn't seem to get my chin out of its way. It popped when it hit, like a balloon breaking.

For a moment the lights went out. The crowd roared like feeding time at the zoo. But the lights came back, spinning and dancing. I danced with them, back, trying to stay up, Johnny after me tigerlike for the kill but with none of the tiger's grace.

I didn't make the mistake of trying to stay away. While his face was still a pink blur, I threw a left at it. Instinct guided it; it straightened him up, not hurting him. He came on.

Somehow I weathered the round.

Next I remember, Doc was waving the smelling salts under my nose, and the ammonia was chasing away the fog with a pitchfork. And it was only the second.

"I'm stopping it, Champ," he said. He still called me Champ; habit, maybe. "Johnny's beating your brains out."

"Stop it," I told him flatly, "and we're through."

He looked at me sad, shaking his head, hoping I was too dazed to know what I was saying. But I meant it, and he knew it. It'd been a long time since we'd been just fighter and manager.

"You got no business in there, Champ," he tried once more. "Not with no twenty-three-year-old kid."

He was right, and I knew it. I was over the hill. For a couple of years now, I'd been just a stepping stone for the champ. A hard stone, though, with fists, and there hadn't been any tough youngsters get by me. The champ paid me off in a fight now and then. There'd been four so far, with me on the receiving end of all of them, but never bad enough to kill off the return.

I was thirty-four. I had been champ for five years, logical contender for two.

I was still a fighter, still the old pro. I knew all the tricks except how to get back the old fire, the old spring in the legs, the sting in the gloves. And here was Johnny, who was good enough to get past me, good enough to take the Champ when he did. There's always one bout a fighter knows is the big one. For me this was it. I couldn't let Johnny get by me, and I couldn't tell Doc why.

How do you tell your best friend that you're afraid your kid brother is a crook?

When the bell rang for the third, Johnny was raging after me, sure he could put me down if he could just catch up. I backpedaled, my legs still rubbery, keeping the left out so he couldn't get set for the finisher. Once in a while I crossed with my right, just to remind him he could still be hurt.

I got hit a few times but nothing serious.

And all the time I was thinking: how had it happened, how had it gone wrong?

But I knew. I told myself: It happened because you weren't smart enough, clever with your fists maybe but dumb in the head. You should've let Doc think for you, like always, but this you had to handle alone.

Johnny was going to be different.

The big purses—we salted them away, Doc and I. They were for Johnny, to put him through school, to make him an engineer, someone who earns money with his brains, not his hands.

He wasn't ever supposed to have anything to do with the fight racket.

A year ago I learned that Johnny was fighting in the sticks, picking up money in the few clubs that TV has left. "You got to stop it," I told him. "Hit the books! How can you learn when you're getting knocked around two-three times a month?"

Johnny looked at me hard and bitter like I never seen him before. "It's good enough for you."

"But not for you. You got to be better. Get back to school, now, like I tell you!"

So maybe it was the wrong thing to say. Who has the words to say it right? To tell him that it's been for him, all of it — the punching and the being hit, the smoky clubs, the long grind of training and eating right. To make him different.

He didn't go back. I was fighting him tonight.

A vicious right caught me high on the head. I didn't even hear the bell.

"Champ — !" Doc began, pleading.

"Don't say it!" I mumbled, spitting out my mouthpiece.

It was funny I should be fighting him, the boy I had been fighting for all these years, and yet it made a kind of sense. I was still fighting for him, fighting to keep him from becoming what he would become unless I stopped him.

I knew now how he must have seen me: hogging the big money, the lights, the cheers, keeping them for myself, not giving him a chance for them. He turned to men who promised them to him. Even then he looked good. Not good like I looked once, you understand, because I learned young and long, and I learned right. Old fighters taught me; experience taught me more.

But Johnny had youth, quick reflexes, strength, and the killer's instinct. It was good, only a champion should have something more, something there are no words for, something like a heart.

The hoodlums picked Johnny up, and it was my fault.

We've got them. There's no way to keep them out of the game, and sometimes they get the whole thing in their dirty hands. That's the bad time that a fighter doesn't like to think about, when the game is hurt, and you play along or you don't eat.

Now was one of the good times, the clean times. We'd helped make it that, Doc and I. We wanted to keep it that way. But let Johnny win this fight, and they were back: promoting, arranging, setting up, fixing....

But mostly it was Johnny.

The fourth and fifth were almost even. I bobbed, I weaved, I rode with the punches, picking them off, taking them on my elbows, my shoulders, giving Johnny a one-two when I could to keep him off balance, clinching when I had to and working him over inside.

I took a few punches; I had to. Johnny wasn't clever, but he was strong. And he wanted to put me away, bad.

He kept yelling at me in the clinches. "What's the matter, yellow-belly? How'd you ever get to be champ? Come on and fight, chicken!"

Johnny! Johnny!

Doc worked feverishly between rounds.

"This ain't so bad," I panted.

"Wait'll the seventh," he mumbled around the swabs between his teeth. "Them eleven years is going to tell."

Yeah. Eleven years is a lot to give away when you're two years over the hill. The Champ's managers had tried to push it first. Johnny was coming up; he had to be taken care of. Besides, it was a natural.

Brother against brother. The greatest match since Cain fought Abel. I told them I'd rather retire.

That was before I heard about Manny. He had Johnny's name on a contract, and I knew what that meant.

He came around, small, dark, quiet, and very dangerous, like always. "Okay," I told him. Doc tried to talk me out of it. He said he wouldn't be in my corner.

It was no use. I knew what I had to do.

I thought I had Johnny in the sixth. I tagged him with some solid left hooks to the body that stung and some rights to the jaw that stopped him and sent him moving away for the first time, respect in his eyes. I thought I had him figured — strictly a bull, no finesse.

I was never a puncher, but I thought maybe I could lay him out.

In the seventh, the roof fell in. Johnny sneaked over another right. The rest of the round I got by on instinct and being too dumb to fall down.

When the bell rang, I had a nose bleed that wasn't important and a slit over the right eye that was. Doc swore under his breath as he tried to patch me up. "I know why you're doing it. I know about the bet. Let it go, Champ. It ain't worth it. He ain't worth it. He's a crook, Champ."

I shook my head, trying to scatter the grayness that hung around it. It wasn't true. Not Johnny. Not yet. It was me who had been wrong, trying to lay out a kid's life for him, trying to make him live a life for me. You can't do that. You got to give a kid some punching room.

Money wasn't enough. Love wasn't enough. You have to give some blood, too.

Manny saw me before the fight. He hinted that there was smart money up, and I'd be smart to go along with it.

"How's it going, Manny?" I asked.

"Two-to-one on Johnny, Champ."

"I never was smart, Manny," I said. "I'll lay you ten grand against Johnny's contract."

"You made a bet, Champ," Manny said quick. He grinned. "You ain't seen the kid. He's got it, like you had it once. And he hates you, Champ. He hates you like poison."

Maybe so, I thought.

In the eighth, I was afraid Manny was right. Johnny was after me, a killer, his eyes red and mean, trying to finish it quick, slamming his fists into me hard and fast. He was hitting me almost at will.

The referee was watching me, careful, and Doc was on his feet, ready to crawl through the ropes. I shook my head at him.

And them I knew I wasn't wrong about Johnny. My hands were at my sides, paralyzed from a body punch; I was weaving my head, trying to get away from the ropes. Johnny started the finisher, and then he got a funny look in his eye, like he remembered when I visited him at school, dressed neat instead of loud, not talking much so he wouldn't be ashamed of me, or putting on the gloves with him when he wasn't much out of diapers....

He pulled the punch. I got away. The bell came like a reprieve.

"This is it," I told Doc. "I get him this round."

Doc laughed, but his eyes were wet. "You ain't getting nobody, Champ."

But I went out for the ninth with new strength in my legs. I had taken everything Johnny had to throw, and I was still up. Doc had my right eye open. I could see again.

As he came rushing for me to end it, I used the opening I had saved from earlier in the bout. I feinted at his bread-basket with a left, and his guard dropped. I crossed with my right as hard as I could throw it.

It hit his chin solid, swiveling his head. His eyes glazed over.

I bored in, throwing the right again and a left and a right, battering his foolish, young head from side to side, muttering, "This is for you, Johnny. This is for you."

They tell me I was still saying it after Johnny was out cold on the canvas. I wouldn't know. I was on my back for two hours.

The surgeon took three stitches in the cut over my right eye, and I laid on the dressing room table feeling very old and very, very tired.

The door opened. Johnny walked in, looking young and fresh and unmarked. "Hello, Champ," he said.

"I'm hanging up my gloves, Johnny," I said. "That was my last fight."

"About time," he said. He stood silent and cleared his throat. "Uh—Manny says you own me."

"Nobody owns you, Johnny," I said. "Doc, give him the contract. Nobody will ever own you again."

Johnny put his hands behind him.

"Who wants it?" he asked quickly. "Somebody's got to handle me. Somebody's got to bring in some money, now you're retired. All I want to know is when do I fight again?"

"Not for a while," I said, and grinned at him, feeling not so old and not tired at all. "Not till you stop being a sucker for a left hand feint."

Maybe there'd be another champion in the family, a champion we could be proud of.

PEST HOUSE

If Kevin Motley had not been almost blind, he wouldn't have been quite so much in the dark later. He might have seen a silvery saucer—about the size of a pizza pan—sail into the house through the open window, tilt as it banked around a corner, and lower itself toward the green-tiled kitchen floor. He might have recognized an interesting fact other saucer observers had overlooked: the saucers were not so fast nor so maneuverable as they seemed. They were small and close; it was a matter of perspective.

Kevin's perspective was all awry. He had been sitting in front of that window for hours, sipping from the bottle beside him every time he thought of Mary Ann. He thought of Mary Ann often. By sunset—a gorgeous splash of red, gold, blue, and purple against the western sky—the sting was almost gone. So was the bourbon. So was his eyesight.

Kevin was not a common lush. He was a man in love. This is meant to cast no aspersions on love but on Mary Ann.

Kevin was a warm-hearted, demonstrative young man with only two ambitions in life: to make enough money so that he would never need to work again and to bring Mary Ann home to this house as a bride. So far he had been eminently unsuccessful at both.

He had never been faced, like some gray-flannel-types, with the hard choice between patched-pants integrity and patched-mind servitude. It was not so much that he had sold his soul to the advertising business; he had given it freely. All he asked of fortune now was to invent a resounding slogan that would assure his success for once and for all.

At the precise moment, however, it had taken everything he could scrape together to make the down payment on this suburban ranch house, that rambled—but not far—across a lot where the bermuda fought a losing battle with the dandelions, the chick weed, and the crab grass. He had the house, a mortgage that would take $100 out of his paycheck for the next 30 years, but no Mary Ann.

Mary Ann, now, was a lovely, long-stemmed creature, whose magnificent dark eyes in the tanned face sparkled with intelligent acquisitiveness. She had a smile that dimpled her cheeks charmingly, and she knew it. She had a disciplined body that did what she told it to without complaining. Her mind did the same.

She knew what she wanted: she wanted security. She was going to wait, with proper caution, until she got it. So far, although she liked Kevin more than she let herself believe, Kevin did not look like security.

All this Kevin knew when he was sober. In a way, it didn't matter; he still loved her.

But it drove him to drink, and this made Mary Ann even less approachable. She did not approve of drinking for good economic reasons.

In the kitchen, where Mary Ann did not preside, the silver saucer sank through the green linoleum squares as if they were sand and made a miniature crater in the floor boards before it stopped.

Idiot! said a small voice in a corner of Kevin's mind. You I keep telling—Jupiter this world is not. At the surface to stop, the anti-grav units we must be using. Women drivers!

Well, here I got you, said another voice.

Here is where?

Where we aimed. The tiny planet. Surveyed it we have. Now contact it is time to make.

Ay! What a lousy navigator and pilot you are. Tangled are my antenna. We are supposed to make contact with what?

With the natives. In case you have forgotten, help we are seeking so that our forces we can rebuild, to Jupiter we can return, and the tyrants we can overthrow.

That I know, dumbhead, but what natives? A thousand times around this world we have been, I swear, and a member of the dominant race we have yet to see. Artifacts like the one in which we are, yes! People, no. Unless the creatures too small to be seen are.

Men! Just because the world small is, small the natives need not be. The reverse! Because of the light gravity, ten-twenty times our size they might be. The size of the artifacts that would help account for.

The size of the artifacts to account for, numskull, would a creature five hundred times our size require!

This no time to argue is. I must get busy with the eggs.

The voices stopped. Kevin was sitting bolt upright in his chair, his eyes wide and incredulous.

He shook his head and stared down at the bottle in his hand. Automatically it started toward his lips, but he stopped it. If he had begun hearing voices, he had reached his limit. Next he would be seeing things.

With infinite care, he screwed the metal cap on the bottle, put it down beside the chair, stood up, waited until the room settled down, and felt his way into the kitchen. The only kind of drink he needed was coffee.

He froze in midstep—a feat worthy of a more sober man. He had almost stepped on a silver saucer about the size of a pizza pan imbedded in a crater in his kitchen floor. And the voices had started again.

Quakes! Shades of Jupiter. For homesick it makes.

For once right you are, lamebrain. The rocking! It delights! But artificial it seems. Is this for our benefit done?

Could it be so? Sensed are we before sensing? If so, a brilliant, sympathetic race have we chanced upon indeed. Up antenna! Rapidly!

Before Kevin's incredulous eyes, a slender silver rod sprouted from the top of the pizza pan. He kicked at it and immediately grabbed his foot and began hopping with the other, screaming and moaning.

The rod was unhurt.

See? Response instantaneous!

Contact let us make!

Kevin forgot about the coffee. He retreated, limping, toward the living room. Just as he reached the bottle and the bottle reached his lips, the voices started again.

A response!

Something I'm pulling in, but feeble. Muddled brain waves. Short circuits. Crossed neurons. Could this member of the race an idiot be?

The bottle gurgled. For a moment the voices faded, and then they came back.

Help the poor thing! Straighten out its mind!

A blue glow grew on the tip of the silver antenna, like St. Elmo's fire. In a moment it detached itself and floated swiftly through the air toward Kevin's head, growing as it came. For a moment Kevin stared at it with shocked eyes, and then he dodged, staggered back, and tripped over the edge of the rug. He sat down heavily.

The fireball dipped with him.

Kevin batted at it ineffectually. "Beat it! Scram!" But he felt nothing, and the fireball, undeterred, passed into his head and was gone.

With an awful clarity, Kevin knew that he was sober. He was more sober than he had ever been. He saw himself with merciless clarity.

He had been drinking for nothing. Mary Ann was what she was, and nothing would change that except maybe a few drinks which she would never take because it might interfere with her self-possession. And he was what he was, and bourbon would only keep him from Mary Ann.

He had been frightfully drunk, sitting here all yesterday afternoon, staring at the sunset, hearing things, seeing things. He had really been loaded! Then he must have passed out and slept until dawn.

He raised himself and looked out the window. Yes, the sky was getting light. No, by Jupiter! it was getting dark. No wonder he was sober; he had slept the day around.

Personally, said a small voice in his head, much improvement I do not see.

A chance give him, dimbrain. For so long he's been a moron, time he needs under control his thoughts to get.

Kevin grabbed at his too sober head and tried under control his thoughts to get. He realized for the first time that he still had the bourbon in his hand. It hadn't been twenty-four hours at all. It had been instantaneous. Outside was the same sunset he had been watching when the voices started.

It wasn't the D.T.'s. He was going mad.

He raised the bottle to his lips and let the fiery liquid burn its way down his throat. It lay in his stomach for a moment, curling, sending out warm tendrils, and then slowly it dissipated.

He was still stone sober.

He took another pull and another. It was useless. He might as well have been drinking distilled water.

Somehow, something had condemned him to cold sobriety.

Now somewhere we are getting. I think perhaps for contact he may be ready.

"No!" Kevin screamed, smashing the bottle against the thing in the kitchen crater. "For contact I'll never be ready!"

He raced for the front door. Before he could get out of the house and out of range, he heard a final remark:

A hydrocarbon! And our storerooms refilling needed. Don't waste a drop.

A race this kind, this considerate, this understanding, too good to be true is.

Kevin had the door open. He fled down the walk, screaming silently.

An hour later he came back down the same walk protesting vigorously to a tall, tanned girl with magnificent dark eyes and a smile that dimpled her cheeks charmingly. But right now she wasn't smiling.

Kevin raised his hand. "I swear that I haven't been drinking. That is," he amended, "that I'm cold sober now. Too sober. It happened, just like I told you. Now I can't even get drunk to forget it."

"I'll believe it when I see it," Mary Ann said, striding briskly toward the door. "The drinking, I mean."

Kevin hung back. "I don't think you should go in."

She turned on him sharply.

"I'm going to prove once and for all, Kevin Motley, that you're going on the wagon or in it. There's nothing in there like this wild story you've been babbling. There couldn't be. It's all in your head."

You're half right anyway, Kevin thought dismally.

Mary Ann opened the door and stalked into the house as if it were already hers.

The creature returns, a voice said. *And with another.*

This one different is. Hard and disciplined is its mind.

"There!" Kevin said triumphantly. "Did you hear that?"

Mary Ann looked at him. "Should I have heard something?"

She had, Kevin thought, *she had. Surely she had. But she wouldn't admit it. She'd rather drive him mad.*

"Well," she said impatiently, "where is it?" Her nose wrinkled. "It smells like a distillery. I wouldn't be surprised at anything you saw."

Kevin pointed at the center of the kitchen floor. "There!" But the crater was gone, and the kitchen floor was smooth and green. "Look! See that tiny silver antenna!" At least that was still there.

"That's a pin!" But she didn't offer to touch it. "Look at that floor. It's filthy!"

There *was* broken glass scattered around, but it wasn't filthy. The bourbon was all gone.

One there is who the verdict of its senses will not accept but believes, and one who its senses will not deny yet refuses to believe.

Dimbrain! The second a female is. Come! Into our suits. Them we cannot perceive directly, but perhaps they can us perceive.

Kevin looked at Mary Ann, but her face was clear and unperturbed. Her head, though, was unnaturally rigid.

The little faker! She was listening. And pretending not to hear! How typical!

"Kevin!" she screamed, jumping back. "Cockroaches! I can't stand the creatures. Step on them!"

On the floor beside the antenna were two flat little many legged silvery things. To Kevin they didn't look like cockroaches, but there was no arguing with Mary Ann. He stepped on them. The sole of his shoe gave.

Ah, the pressure! The beautiful sensation! So good I have not felt since Jupiter we left.

The goodness, the thoughtfulness of these creatures....

Kevin lifted his foot. The silver things were unhurt, but his shoe had dents in it. He went to the utility room and took down a hammer from its place on the peg board. He knelt down vindictively beside the little creatures and hit one. The hammer bounced off harmlessly.

There! Again! Exquisite! I can't stand it!

Where! Where! What is it?

Kevin swung the hammer in a vicious arc, but he only succeeded in driving the shiny thing into the linoleum. It lifted itself out with no difficulty. Kevin whacked it again and made another dent. He took a swing at the needlelike antenna. It made his hand sting so bad that he dropped the hammer. The antenna did not move.

He looked up helplessly. Mary Ann was gone. He ran into the living room. The front door stood open. He rein to it. Mary Ann was halfway down the walk to the car.

"Mary Ann!"

She turned toward him a face that was cool and unruffled. "I simply can't stand dirty insects. I won't go in that house again, Kevin, until you get rid of them."

"Get rid of them!" Kevin wailed. "How?"

She slid into the car, slammed the door, and leaned her head out the window.

"Try insect powder. If that doesn't work, get an exterminator. If that doesn't work, get another girl." The car pulled away from the curb.

It was Kevin's car, but he couldn't think of anything to say. Mary Ann was like that. She borrowed things.

Kevin turned and stared moodily at the brown ranch house that was to have been his and Mary Ann's honeymoon cottage. Now it was a white elephant that he had to keep meeting the payments on, a pest house taken over by telepathic insects that he couldn't even believe in.

If the voices in his head could be believed, they were refugees from Jupiter seeking some kind of help from Earth.

Refugees from Jupiter! he scoffed.

He needed his head examined. He needed a drink!

He went through the front door and marched through the living room. He didn't want to go into the kitchen, but that was where the bottle was. The two little silvery shapes were scurrying about the floor, but Kevin ignored them loftily and went to the cabinet above the sink. He took out an unopened fifth of bourbon. Methodically he stripped off the plastic strip and unscrewed the cap. He raised it to his lips and let it gurgle down his throat, neat.

He waited for a feeling of peace to sweep over him. In vain. He took another pull on the bottle. Still nothing. Impatiently he killed a third of it before he lowered it.

The spell was still working. These happy insects, these jovial Jovians had removed his ability to react to alcohol. With that blue ball of fire they had given him a cure to end all cures. He could drink all day and it wouldn't matter. Why drink?

Kevin sighed, capped the bottle, and put it away. He looked under the sink, the insecticide was in a round can with a flat, pry-up lid. The label said:

POISON
Keep away from children and pets.
Sprinkle around edges of area where insects are found.
Active ingredients: sodium fluoride and barium fluosili-
cate.

He sprinkled the powder in a circle around the tiny antenna and the bright bugs. Then he perched on a stool, put his chin in his hands, and watched them. One of them blundered into the circle of powder and stopped. In a moment the other came rushing to its side.

Kevin watched them, but they did not move. He sighed a giant sigh. He had been afraid that his life was ruined, but perhaps after all it was only crippled. It was going to be all right.

He realized suddenly that he hadn't heard a voice since he came back into the house. Or was it that he had heard them and hadn't listened?

With the thought the voices returned loud and clear:

Whoopee!

Can't over — over — everst'mate symp'thy 'n' gen'rosity of natives. Whee!

You know what? You're drunk!

So 're you!

True, true. As gov'nor of Noth Jup'ter said to gov'nor of South Jup'ter, "A long time between snifters it is."

Seri-seri-seri'sly. Trace element this is for eggs. Now to thorax's content can hatch.

Kevin stared numbly at the tiny insects. Everything he did turned out wrong. The nasty little things had cost him Mary Ann. They were taking over his mortgaged house. They had even taken away his ability to forget his troubles.

Tears of self-pity sprang into his eyes. He dashed them away. He'd get them, that's what he'd do. He'd call an exterminator. He didn't care if they had to fumigate the whole house.

He left the disgusting little drunks nuzzling the sodium fluoride and the barium fluosilicate and went to the phone. In the phone book, the exterminators were listed under "pest control service." Under that heading was a page of phone numbers and advertisements.

One ad drew his eyes. It was headed:

DEATH SPECIALIST
We don't "control"—We KILL!
One application with a one-year written guarantee to eliminate moths, silverfish, carpet beetles, roaches, water-bugs, etc.
AJAX EXTERMINATORS
A.J. "Andy" Andrews, Mgr.

The "etc.," Kevin decided — that's what he had.

Andy was a red-eyed whiskery middle-aged man. He drove up in front of the house in an old pick-up. It had his motto in faded lettering on the side.

Kevin, sitting gloomily on the front porch, didn't think he looked much like a death specialist.

"You the guy with the bugs?" Andy asked.

Kevin nodded slowly. "Come on."

He followed him through the door and started toward the kitchen.

Andy stopped suddenly and looked at Kevin. "What'd you say?" he asked in amazement.

"I didn't say anything," Kevin said.

"Somebody said something," Andy insisted stubbornly, "and they're still sayin' it."

Kevin listened for a moment.

Never again! Ne-ver a-gain!

From this one you're not even recovered, and about the next time you're talking already.

Go away. There's an idiot in your suit. In peace let me die.

"Just don't listen," Kevin said off-handedly. "That's what I do. They're a couple of lushes anyway."

"I don't want to listen," Andrew wailed, "but I can't help myself."

Kevin looked at him soberly. "You need a drink."

"Yes, I do," Andy said fervently.

As they walked into the kitchen, Kevin said casually, "There's the bugs." The insecticide was all gone now except for a few grains, and one of the bugs sucked these up and scurried back to the antenna to which the other clung.

"Now I do need a drink," Andy said faintly.

Kevin got the bottle out of the cabinet. "What are they?"

"Why do you ask me?" Andy said. "They're your bugs." He grabbed the bottle out of Kevin's hands.

"Silverfish?" Kevin ventured.

Andy gurgled. Then he gasped. "Never saw anything like them in my life." He gurgled again.

"Well, can you get rid of them?"

When Andy answered his voice was less precise and more confident. "Never found any I couldn't."

Kevin looked pessimistic. "Yeah? Everything I've tried has been just what they needed."

"Never saw a bug," Andy said, "that could live in a house full of hydrogen cyanide." He gurgled again. The more he gurgled, the more confident he got. "I'll wipe 'em out." Finally he said triumphantly, "I've stop' hearin' voices."

Kevin eyed the bottle. It was almost empty. By this time Andy had probably stopped hearing everything.

When Kevin looked back at the bugs, he noticed the ball of blue fire growing on the tip of the tiny silver antenna. It broke free as he stopped it and began floating through the air.

"Watch it!" he shouted, and pushed Andy aside.

"Wha'! Wha'!" Andy spluttered as the bourbon gushed down his whiskery chin. "Look wha' you made me do!" Then his bleary eyes focused on the ball of fire. It was two feet from his head. His eyes widened; his mouth opened, but no sound came out. At the last moment, he tried to dodge, but it was too late. The fireball passed into his head and disappeared.

A look of startled sobriety tightened Andy's loose features. "What hit me?"

"You've just been struck sober," Kevin said glumly. "It happens around here."

Andy shuddered. "A horrible condition. What did it?"

Kevin nodded toward the floor. "They did."

"Them?" Andy glowered at the bugs. "That does it! I'm gonna really give it to 'em. First, though, I need another drink."

Kevin shook his head. "That was the last in the house. Wouldn't do any good anyhow. It'd be like pouring it down the drain. The condition is permanent."

Andy stared at Kevin with undisguised horror. "You mean— ? Never again—?"

Kevin nodded in gloomy sympathy. "It happened to me, too."

Andy glared malevolently at the bugs. "Even if they weren't bugs, anybody'd do that deserves to die. What they did I wouldn't do to a cockroach."

"What's stopping you?" Kevin asked.

"Nothin'!" Andy spat out fiercely. Now he looked like a death specialist.

He got rolls of masking tape out of his pick-up. He and Kevin went through the house taping windows, doors, and miscellaneous cracks. Andy left a small opening beneath a front window. Into this he inserted a hose attached to a large metal gas cylinder. He turned a valve. The hose began to hiss. He leaned back against the pick-up, smiling the hard smile of the victorious. "There, you little devils," he said, "see how you like that!"

A brief qualm clutched Kevin's stomach with an icy hand. The little tykes. They had come all the way from Jupiter. Looking for help. And what did they find? Killers. They hadn't hurt anybody—not much, anyhow. Now they were dying, millions of miles from home.

The back window drew him irresistibly. He stared through it into the kitchen. Suddenly he stiffened, straightened, waved imperiously at Andy. Silently, as the exterminator bent to the window, Kevin pointed at the kitchen floor.

The bugs had split apart. Out of shiny silver halves came two fluorescent purple bugs.

Andy scratched his bristly chin with a yellow thumb-nail. "I don't get it."

"Spacesuits," Kevin muttered.

"But—"

"Listen!"

The beautiful air. The beautiful sympathy. The beautiful people. Again freely we can breath.

With a suitable environment to provide us — generosity without parallel it is. Now our children in a proper fashion we can raise.

So much to do yet. This flimsy artifact we must strengthen. When the antigravity we reverse so that the eggs will hatch, it can the weight withstand. Then the long way back to Jupiter will have just begun.

At last Kevin admitted the truth to himself. The bugs were from Jupiter, that huge, cold fifth planet from the sun. That's why they were so little. In Jupiter's gravity nothing could grow big. And they had to be tough to withstand the pressure of Jupiter's massive atmosphere.

They had fled from their home for reasons that were probably political. They came to Earth for sanctuary. Now they were going to raise an Army — really raise it — and return.

With their luck, Kevin didn't see how they could miss.

Andrew suggested, without much hope, "We could break a window."

Kevin sighed. "It would turn out to be just what they needed. Go turn off the cyanide. Seal up the hole. Send me the bill."

Andy shrugged. "It's your house." He paused. "Or was."

Kevin said sadly, "The next payment is due Wednesday."

By Monday Mary Ann could stand it no longer. She came looking for Kevin.

Kevin met her in the front yard. It wasn't a front yard any more. Where the bermuda had fought a losing battle with the dandelions, the chick weed, and the crab grass, there was now a paved parking lot. In the center of it was a tall pillar. On the pillar was a blue neon sign:

SEE THE MARTIANS!
SEE their flying saucer!
HEAR their telepathic conversation!
WATCH them build cities, factories, spaceships, raise
children, drill armies.
Admission $1

The parking lot was crammed with cars. At every window of the house, a wooden balcony held bleachers and every bleacher seat held a spectator, his eyes peering in the window.

"Thank goodness you brought back the car," Kevin said.

Mary Ann stared up at the sign. "What is all this?"

"They're really from Jupiter," Kevin said apologetically, "But nobody has ever heard of Jupiter."

"Are you making money?"

"Faster than I can get it to the bank. That's why I've missed the car. The paving and the balconies cost almost a thousand dollars, and I've already got that back. At night the government takes over for another thousand. They want to find out how the anti-gravity works. I don't think they'll have much luck, though.

"The bugs told me how to make that blue fireball—the sober-upper—but they said we couldn't understand the anti-gravity. They were right."

Dazedly Mary Ann asked, "What are you going to do with it—the sober-upper?"

"Oh, I'm patenting the thing. No bar should be without one. The strength can be cut down. Then it isn't permanent. Don't you want to look?"

For a moment Mary Ann held back, but cupidity won over caution. She walked to a balcony that had just been vacated. She bent over and peered through the picture window. The living room was crawling with florescent purple insects. "Ugh!" she said.

"They've got a way to speed up the breeding process," Kevin said. "Look! They're building."

In the center of the room a group of silver buildings was growing into a city. "The walls of the house," Kevin said, "are coated with that stuff. Windows, too, except there it's transparent That's a favor to me. The government scientists say that they can't even scratch it with their sharpest drills. They think it's some collapsed metal—matter as it exists under the pressure of Jupiter. The bugs are mining it miles down and converting it in the crawl space. Inside there, the air pressure is twenty times ours."

Mary Ann said, "The bugs—they'll take over."

"Not a chance," Kevin said. "It's just too much trouble. They have to expend too much energy to stay alive. There's Neptune, Saturn, and Uranus—giant, cold worlds like their own—that they can colonize in comfort. No, they're here because no one would ever think of looking here for them."

Ah! The cold, unhappy one has returned.

Poor creature! Something can't we do?

Kevin's eyes widened. "Did you hear that?"

Mary Ann looked innocent. She did it very well. "Hear what?"

"They were talking about you!"

Mary Ann frowned. "I thought you were on the wagon. If you're going to—"

"Look out!" Kevin shouted.

The green fireball came though the window as if there were nothing there. It passed into Mary Ann's head and disappeared.

Mary Ann's controlled features relaxed.

She smiled, really smiled, Kevin realized, for the first time. Her magnificent eyes widened, looked hungrily at Kevin. "Swee'hear'!" she said. "I'm jus' crazy 'bout you!"

"Hey!" Kevin shouted at the house. "You've got to do something about this."

Nobody paid any attention.

"Worry too much," said Mary Ann, trying to kiss him and planting a red smear of lipstick on his nose. "Don' worry. Jus' have fun! Whoopee!"

Kevin sighed and swung Mary Ann into his arms. She lay there, lasciviously boneless, her arms draped around his neck, her lips nibbling at his ear lobe.

Those darned bugs! They always overdid everything.

ABOUT THE AUTHOR

James Gunn is the author of more than thirty books, including the Hugo Award-winning nonfiction work *Isaac Asimov: The Foundations of Science Fiction* and the novel *The Immortals*, on which the television series *The Immortal* was based. Other novels include *The Listeners, The Joy Makers,* and *Kampus.* He also has collaborated with other authors, most notably with Jack Williamson on *Star Bridge.* He was named a Grand Master by the Science Fiction and Fantasy Writers of America in 2007.

Mr. Gunn is also the editor of a series of anthologies tracing the history of science fiction, *The Road to Science Fiction,* and is a past president of The Science Fiction Writers of America. He is professor emeritus of English and was the founding director of the Center for the Study of Science Fiction at the University of Kansas. He is the winner of the Pilgrim Award for lifetime achievement in science fiction scholarship, and is a past president of the Science Fiction Research Association. He lives in Lawrence, Kansas.

More books from James Gunn are available at:
www.ReAnimus.com/store/?author=James%20Gunn

ReAnimus Press

The Immortals, by James Gunn
Info/buy:

James Gunn's masterpiece about a human fountain of youth.

Transcendental - The Trilogy, by James Gunn
Info/buy:

Not all the pilgrims are what they seem on their quest for transcendence

Transcendental, by James Gunn
Info/buy:

Not all the pilgrims are what they seem on their quest for transcendence

Transgalactic, by James Gunn
Info/buy:

Riley and Asha set out to change the galaxy--if only they can find each other.

Transformation, by James Gunn
Info/buy:

Third in the Transcendental Machine trilogy...

Pilgrims to Transcendence, by James Gunn
Info/buy:

Not all the pilgrims are what they seem on their quest for transcendence

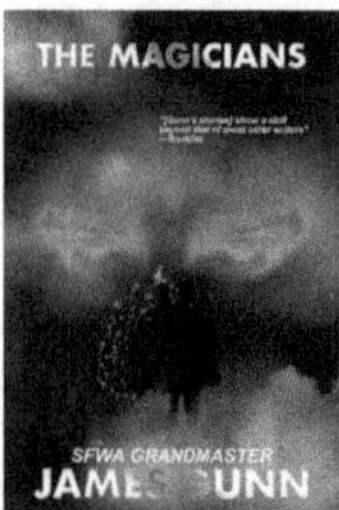

The Magicians, by James Gunn
Info/buy:

Can a band of social rejects save humanity from the Black Magician?

Kampus, by James Gunn
Info/buy:

Tomorrow's students invent the ultimate revolution

The Dreamers, by James Gunn
Info/buy:

When computers do everything and most humans live a fantasy life, a new human overseer is needed.

The Joy Machine, by James Gunn
Info/buy:

Jim Gunn's Star Trek novel

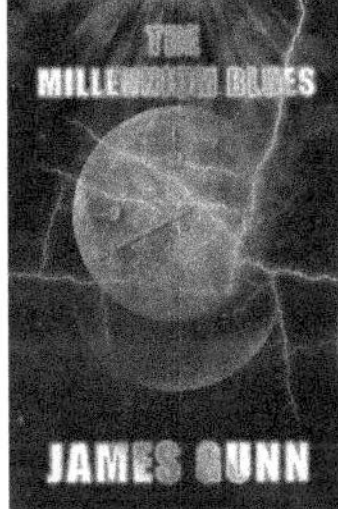

The Millennium Blues, by James Gunn

Info/buy:

The End of the World is nigh...

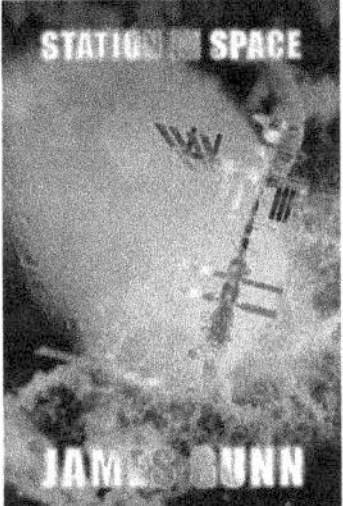

Station in Space, by James Gunn

Info/buy:

Mankind begins to conquer to last frontier

Future Imperfect, by James Gunn

Info/buy:

Infinite possibilities of unknown worlds from a Grand Master of SF

The Witching Hour, by James Gunn

Info/buy:

Science and science fiction meet magic...

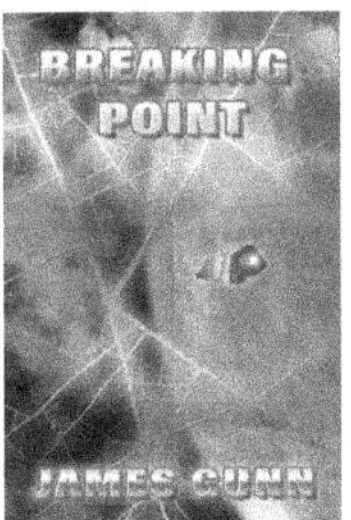

Breaking Point, by James Gunn

Info/buy:

What do you do when you're pushed to the breaking point?

The Burning, by James Gunn
Info/buy:

Is it science, love, or magic?

Some Dreams Are Nightmares, by James Gunn
Info/buy:

Some of mankind's great dreams have unforessen consequences...

Crisis!, by James Gunn
Info/buy:

Johnson has to save the future through time travel, but his memory isn't great...

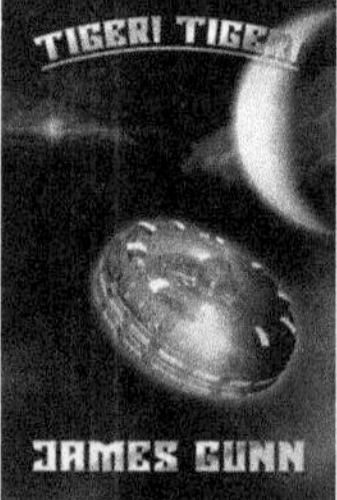

Tiger! Tiger!, by James Gunn
Info/buy:

An object that shouldn't be there passed within a hundred yards of the space station.

The End of the Dreams, by James Gunn
Info/buy:

Three short novels about space, happiness, and immortality.

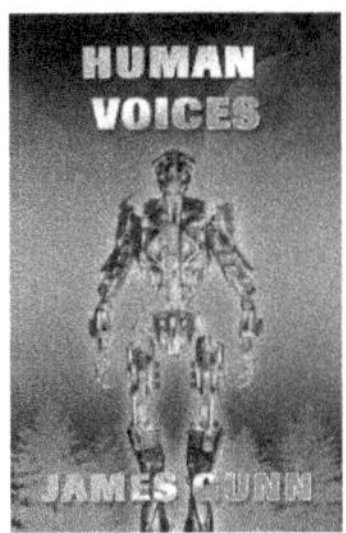

Human Voices, by James Gunn
Info/buy:

An enthralling collection of the SFWA Grandmaster's later stories

Isaac Asimov: The Foundation of Science Fiction, by James Gunn
Info/buy:

The Discovery of the Future: The Ways Science Fiction Developed, by James Gunn
Info/buy:

Man and the Future, by James Gunn
Info/buy:

Speculations on Speculation: Theories of Science Fiction, by James Gunn and Matthew Candelaria
Info/buy:

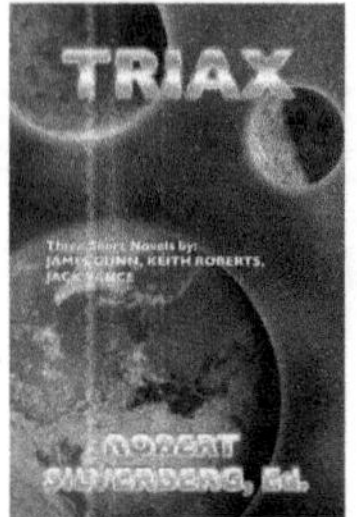

Triax, by Robert Silverberg, James Gunn, Keith Roberts, Jack Vance

Info/buy:

Three original short science fiction novels by legends in the genre

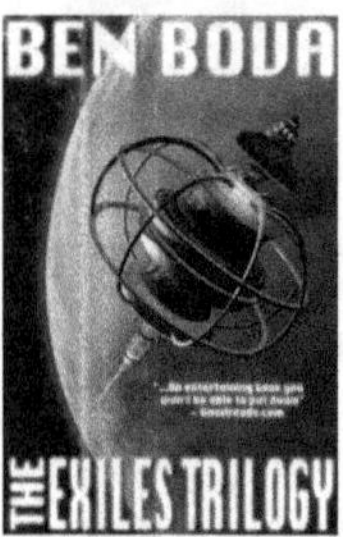

The Exiles Trilogy, by Ben Bova

Info/buy:

When all the best of Earth's scientists are exiled to a space station, they decide to embark on an even grander adventure to the stars. An epic trilogy in one volume.

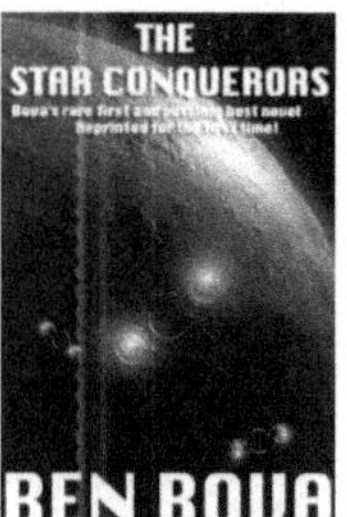

The Star Conquerors (Collectors' Edition), by Ben Bova

Info/buy:

Special Collectors' Edition! Six time Hugo winner Ben Bova's most sought-after novel is now an ebook with the original Mel Hunter cover and an essay from Ben on the history of the book!

The Star Conquerors (Standard Edition), by Ben Bova

Info/buy:

Six time Hugo winner Ben Bova's most sought-after novel is back in print!

Colony, by Ben Bova

Info/buy:

Island One is a celestial utopia, and David Adams is its most perfect creation. But David is a prisoner, destined to spend his life in an island-sized cylinder orbiting a doomed home planet. David has a plan—one that will ultimately save humanity... or destroy it.

The Kinsman Saga, by Ben Bova

Info/buy:

Chet Kinsman is an astronaut ace who has done everything in space—including committing the first murder. Kinsman has to confront his hidden past and decide Earth's destiny, in a desperate countdown to nuclear annihilation.

Star Watchmen, by Ben Bova

Info/buy:

Mankind rules a giant galactic empire, but not all the worlds are pleased. Can the Star Watch prevent a revolt?

As on a Darkling Plain, by Ben Bova

Info/buy:

Dr. Sidney Lee races against time to prevent the huge alien machines on Titan from destroying mankind.

The Winds of Altair, by Ben Bova

Info/buy:

Altair VI isn't making it easy to Terraform!

Test of Fire, by Ben Bova

Info/buy:

A small group of survivors fight to rebuild civilization after the Earth is devastated by a huge solar flare.

The Weathermakers, by Ben Bova
Info/buy:

After conquering everything else, the last frontier was... controlling Mother Nature! By the award-winning hard SF author of the Grand Tour series.

The Dueling Machine, by Ben Bova
Info/buy:

Civilized, harmless virtual reality dueling has replaced all physical conflict — everything from punching someone over a personal insult to interstellar warfare... until a madman dictator of a small empire finds a way to cheat, and use the dueling machine to take over the galaxy!

The Multiple Man, by Ben Bova
Info/buy:

As the President is speaking inside an auditorium in Boston, the President's Press Secretary discovers a body in an alley outside: The body of the President.

Escape!, by Ben Bova
Info/buy:

No end to Danny's sentence, watched by a sentient computer, and no way out of the escape-proof prison, there was only one thing to do...

Forward in Time, by Ben Bova
Info/buy:

Get ready for a series of future shocks from the award-winning Ben Bova!

Maxwell's Demons, by Ben Bova

Info/buy:

Science fiction and science fact, humor and adventure, all await when you enter the unpredictable world of... MAXWELL'S DEMONS

Twice Seven, by Ben Bova

Info/buy:

Ben Bova's universe is always more than the sum of its parts...

The Astral Mirror, by Ben Bova

Info/buy:

Here are a dozen and a half views of the world, past present and future, as seen through the Astral Mirror....

The Story of Light, by Ben Bova

Info/buy:

In this all-encompassing work, Ben Bova explores the subject of light and shows how it has shaped every aspect of our existence.

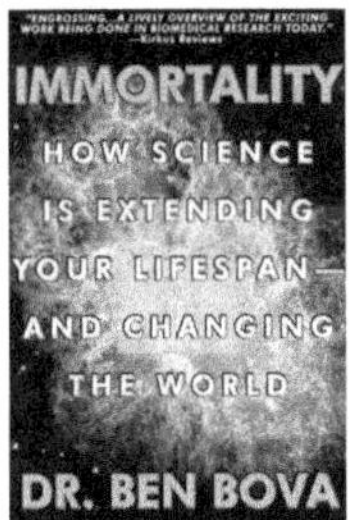

Immortality, by Ben Bova

Info/buy:

Dr. Bova explores the future effects of science and technology on the human life span. Death will no longer be the inevitable end of life.

Space Travel - A Science Fiction Writer's Guide, by Ben Bova

Info/buy:

An indispensible tool for all science fiction writers, Space Travel explains the science you need to help you make your fiction plausible.

The Craft of Writing Science Fiction that Sells, by Ben Bova

Info/buy:

Learn how to write SF from the master! Ben Bova, best-selling author and six-time Hugo Award winner for Best Editor explains step by step all the elements you need to write professionally selling science fiction.

Walls and Wonders, by S. R. Algernon

Info/buy:

Hugo finalist... If Hemingway wrote P.K.Dick-ian science fiction short stories...

The Unborn, by Brian Herbert

Info/buy:

In the summer of 2097, Riggio wakes up with amnesia--and his lover dead in their bed.

The Assassination of Billy Jeeling, by Brian Herbert

Info/buy:

From the New York Times Bestselling author of the DUNE series comes a spectacular science fiction novel.

Phoenix Without Ashes, by Harlan Ellison and Edward Bryant

Info/buy:

Co-written with Harlan Ellison and based on the award-winning script, the story of mankind's last salvation gone awry.

Bloom, by Wil McCarthy

Info/buy:

In 2106, microscopic machine/creatures escape their creators to populate the inner solar system with a wild, deadly ecology all their own, pushing the tattered remnants of humanity out into the cold and dark of the outer planets. Seven astronauts must embark on mankind's boldest venture yet—the perilous journey home to infected Earth!

Aggressor Six, by Wil McCarthy

Info/buy:

An alien armada from the center of Orion makes its deadly way through the galaxy, destroying all human life in the process, and only Marine Corporal Kenneth Jonson and the Aggressor Six team can stop the onslaught.

Murder in the Solid State, by Wil McCarthy

Info/buy:

David Sanger, an ambitious young physicist, attends a party at which a pompous older scientist, who just happens to have thwarted the younger man's innovative ideas, is murdered. Suddenly it is not just David's career, but his life that is at stake. Are his ideas that important? Who's out to stop David from changing the world?

Flies from the Amber, by Wil McCarthy

Info/buy:

Forty light years from earth, the colonists on the world of Unua have somehow managed to keep civilization struggling on, despite twice daily earthquakes...

Vengeance of Orion, by Ben Bova

Info/buy:

Orion must travel back in time to change history and save Troy from the Greek army, or lose the only woman he has ever loved.

Orion in the Dying Time, by Ben Bova

Info/buy:

Time-traveling into the era of the dinosaurs, Orion must save the very fabric of spacetime from the satanic reptilian leader of the saurians.

Orion and the Conqueror, by Ben Bova

Info/buy:

Orion travels to the time of Alexander the Great, battling to save the future of mankind, and his own soul.

Orion Among the Stars, by Ben Bova

Info/buy:

The superhuman, time-traveling Orion leads interstellar warriors in a galactic war among the gods themselves.

The Starcrossed, by Ben Bova

Info/buy:

A stinging SFnal, futuristic satire on the TV industry, based a bit on reality.

To Save The Sun, by Ben Bova and A. J. Austin

Info/buy:

Earth's sun will soon explode, unless a massive engineering effort can save it.

The Gate of Worlds, by Robert Silverberg

Info/buy:

An Alternate History adventure in the modern day Turkish and Aztec Empires.

Conquerors from the Darkness, by Robert Silverberg

Info/buy:

Long after the earth has been conquered by aliens and flooded, Dovirr Stargan longs to become one of the pirate-like Sea Lords.

Time of the Great Freeze, by Robert Silverberg

Info/buy:

ICE AGE--NEW YORK CITY 2650 A.D. UNDERGROUND!

Enter a Soldier. Later: Another, by Robert Silverberg

Info/buy:

Hugo Award Winner, from an SF Grandmaster!

The Longest Way Home, by Robert Silverberg

Info/buy:

The planet's locals have risen up, trapping young Joseph thousands of miles from home.

The Alien Years, by Robert Silverberg

Info/buy:

"The ultimate alien invasion novel"

Tower of Glass, by Robert Silverberg

Info/buy:

Aliens have sent a mysterious signal, which Simeon Krug is determined to answer.

Hot Sky at Midnight, by Robert Silverberg

Info/buy:

Greed comes home to roost in a future Earth and her colonies, and the renegades look to take over. One of Silverberg's finest.

The New Springtime, by Robert Silverberg

Info/buy:

Humans emerge to reclaim Earth after the Long Winter, but never anticipated what awaits...

Shadrach in the Furnace, by Robert Silverberg

Info/buy:

Meet the new Khan! Soon to be immortal... A Hugo and Nebula Award Finalist novel from a Grand Master of science fiction.

The Stochastic Man, by Robert Silverberg

Info/buy:

Lew Nichols uses statistical methods to guess trends--then meets a man who can actually see the future.

Thorns, by Robert Silverberg

Info/buy:

Beauty and the Beast in the solar colonies

Kingdoms of the Wall, by Robert Silverberg

Info/buy:

Not all is at it seems on pilgrimages up the gigantic mountain called The Wall

Challenge for a Throne, by Robert Silverberg

Info/buy:

The real life Game of Thrones, and basis George R.R. Martin used for the GoT series.

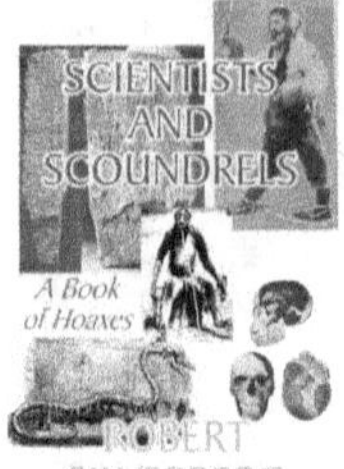

Scientists and Scoundrels, by Robert Silverberg

Info/buy:

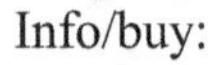

A good-humored tour through scientific frauds and how they were exposed.

Deep Quarry, by John E. Stith

Info/buy:

A private eye uncovers a long-buried starship...that's still occupied.

Manhattan Transfer, by John E. Stith

Info/buy:

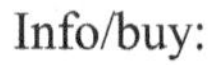

Aliens kidnap Manhattan; read all about it!

Reunion on Neverend, by John E. Stith

Info/buy:

A man returning for a high school reunion on a distant colony finds an old flame in trouble—trouble that he's uniquely qualified to deal with.

Redshift Rendezvous, by John E. Stith

Info/buy:

One man must stop starship hijackers from using an unusual starship to plunder a wealthy colony.

Memory Blank, by John E. Stith

Info/buy:

Cal Donley regains consciousness on the beautiful orbital colony Daedalus—but Cal doesn't remember leaving Earth, or his name or the past dozen years!

Reckoning Infinity, by John E. Stith

Info/buy:

A riveting exploration of what it means to be an alien... Explorers inside a moon-sized alien ship must find its secrets before it kills them.

Death Tolls, by John E. Stith

Info/buy:

A great science fiction mystery: Dan sees the telecast from Mars where his brother dies—and it's not an accident. Why is a certain reporter uncannily at each disaster so quickly?

Scapescope, by John E. Stith

Info/buy:

Brother Sammy Wants YOU! In prison. For something you haven't done yet.

All for Naught, by John E. Stith

Info/buy:

Nick Naught, private eye, walks down some strange mean streets, in an action-packed comedy set in the future.

In Search of the Big Bang, by John Gribbin

Info/buy:

For Big Bang Theory fans, don't miss this indispensable guide! :) `A remarkably readable guide to the mysteries of cosmic creation' —Nature

Cosmic Coincidences, by John Gribbin and Martin Rees

Info/buy:

A provocative search through space and time for a cosmic blueprint—and the source of life in the universe.

Q is for Quantum, by John Gribbin

Info/buy:

A comprehensive encyclopedia of quantum physics.

Ice Age, by John and Mary Gribbin

Info/buy:

The theory that came in from the cold...

In Search of the Double Helix, by John Gribbin

Info/buy:

Unraveling the mystery of life on earth...

The Living Labyrinth, by Ian Stewart and Tim Poston

Info/buy:

Sam, Jane, Felix, Elzabet, Tinka & Marco go quantum jumping on their path to galactic citizenship, only to end up in a very strange place indeed!

Rock Star, by Tim Poston and Ian Stewart

Info/buy:

The awesome sequel to The Living Labyrinth. It's all fun and games with syntei until they fall into the wrong hands...

Wheelers, by Ian Stewart and Jack Cohen

Info/buy:

Alien artifacts found on Callisto...

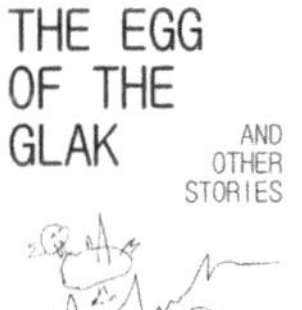

The Egg of the Glak, by Harvey Jacobs

Info/buy:

Some of Harvey's best, believably fantastical short stories.

A Guide to Barsoom, by John Flint Roy

Info/buy:

THE OFFICIAL, DEFINITIVE GUIDE TO EDGAR RICE BURROUGH'S BARSOOM. Everything there is to know about John Carter of Mars and his world — the people, places and things, with maps and fully illustrated.

Jewels of the Dragon, by Allen L. Wold
Info/buy:

The greatest of treasures awaits... on the deadliest of planets.

Crown of the Serpent, by Allen L. Wold
Info/buy:

In farthest space lie hidden fortunes... and unknown enemies.

Lair of the Cyclops, by Allen L. Wold
Info/buy:

Rickard Braeth and friends must find the galaxy's secret—before it's used to destroy everything!

The Planet Masters, by Allen L. Wold
Info/buy:

Troubleshooter Larson McCade searches for the alien Book of Aradka on the planet Seltique, and may find more than he bargained for.

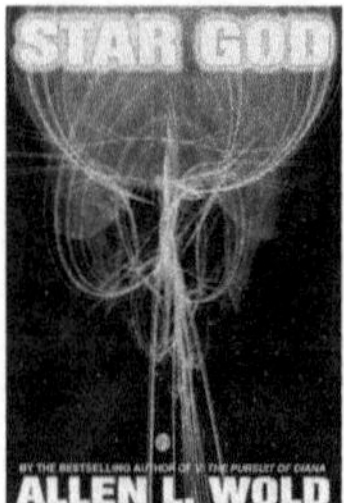 

Star God, by Allen L. Wold
Info/buy:

There is a strange force at work in the universe. It must be stopped. But first, it must be understood.

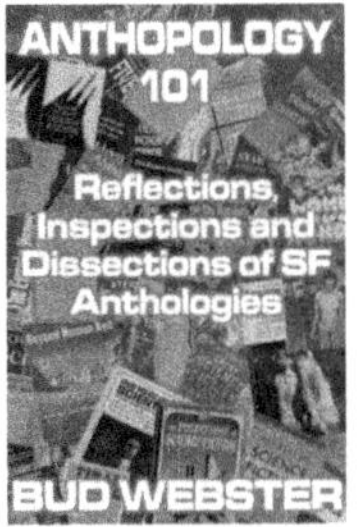

Anthopology 101: Reflections, Inspections and Dissections of SF Anthologies, by Bud Webster

Info/buy:

Bud expertly dissects the great SF anthologies. A must for writers and SF fans.

Woman Without a Shadow, by Karen Haber

Info/buy:

War Minstrels #1. Kayla, an extraordinarily gifted young telepath, is on the run after challenging the most powerful families on her home planet, who've tried to take everything from her.

The Sweet Taste of Regret, by Karen Haber

Info/buy:

Live anywhere you want... in any time... A collection of Karen Haber's best short fiction.

The Science of Middle-earth, by Henry Gee

Info/buy:

How did Frodo's mithril coat ward off the fatal blow of an orc? Can Balrogs fly? Nature editor Dr. Henry Gee explains how. A must-read for Tolkien fans.

Commencement, by Roby James

Info/buy:

The Sting was what made Ronica McBride special—now she was crashed on an unknown planet without it.

Xenostorm: Rising, by Brian Clegg

Info/buy:

14 year old Davy finds himself facing a powerful underground group who have lived for hundreds of years—and want to see him dead. The future of human existence is in the balance...

The Cure for Everything, by Severna Park

Info/buy:

Finding the cure for all diseases comes with a heavy price. Nebula Award winner!

Ghosts of Engines Past, by Sean McMullen

Info/buy:

Award winning steampunk from a master!

Colours of the Soul, by Sean McMullen

Info/buy:

Why are cheetahs the most perfect of creatures? Besides because they're cats, that is... Cool, mind-blowing stories from a master.

The Gilded Basilisk, by Chet Gottfried

Info/buy:

Add a basilisk, a dragon, and weirdragons to the mix-up of a theft going from bad to worse: Friends become enemies and enemies friends, wars loom, and the intrigues threaten the fate of two kingdoms.

Einar and the Cursed City, by Chet Gottfried

Info/buy:

Sixteen-year-old Einar enters Jorghaven for dueling and desserts, but a curse has changed everyone except Barbara Bloodbath, who needs his help to free the city!

Neon Twilight, by Edward Bryant

Info/buy:

Neon Twilight by Edward Bryant : Three wonderful space opera stories, including Ed's Berserker story!

Particle Theory, by Edward Bryant

Info/buy:

Particle Theory by Edward Bryant : A collection of many of Ed's best works, including two Nebula Award winning short stories.

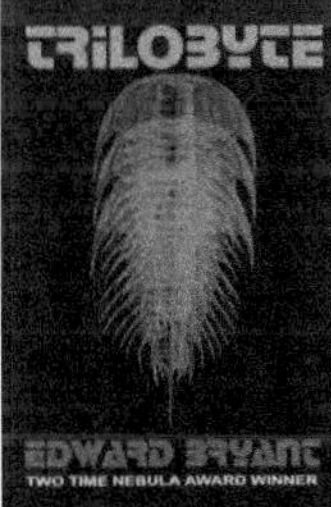 

Trilobyte, by Edward Bryant

Info/buy:

A trio of twisted little tales from the master of twistedness.

Cinnabar, by Edward Bryant

Info/buy:

In the city at the center of time, paradox is just another urban renewal project.

Predators and Other Stories, by Edward Bryant

Info/buy:

Troubling tales as only Ed Bryant can tell. Don't miss the author introductions!

Timeshare, by Joshua Dann

Info/buy:

Have you ever wished you could go back to the good old days? At Timeshare Unlimited, you can.

Bug Jack Barron, by Norman Spinrad

Info/buy:

GET SET FOR THE BEST THING THAT EVER HAPPENED TO YOU! The banned book is back! You've heard of it, now you can read it! Lover and hero, Jack Barron, troubleshooter and media god of the Bug Jack Barron Show, has one last chance to hit it big when he meets Benedict Howards, the power-mad man with the secret to immortality. A Hugo and Nebula Award finalist!

The Void Captain's Tale, by Norman Spinrad

Info/buy:

Symbiotically linked to her ship, Void Pilot Dominique Alia Wu senses something transcendent in the void...

The Last Hurrah of the Golden Horde, by Norman Spinrad

Info/buy:

"One of the greatest collections of science fiction short stories ever" — Goodreads.com

Costigan s Needle, by Jerry Sohl
Info/buy:

What really was Dr. Costigan's tool for medical research? Where did the eye of the needle actually lead to?

The Mars Monopoly, by Jerry Sohl
Info/buy:

One of the famous Ace Doubles, with the wonderful original cover, The Mars Monopoly still stands today as a great, fun story in the classic style.

One Against Herculum, by Jerry Sohl
Info/buy:

One of the famous Ace Doubles, with the wonderful original cover, One Against Herculum remains a fast-paced, fun story that you'll really enjoy.

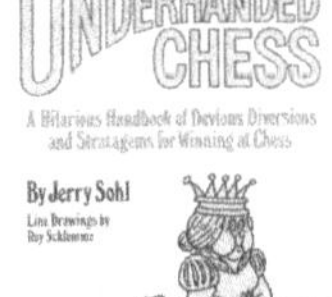

Underhanded Chess, by Jerry Sohl
Info/buy:

A hilarious handbook of devious diversions and stratagems for winning at chess.

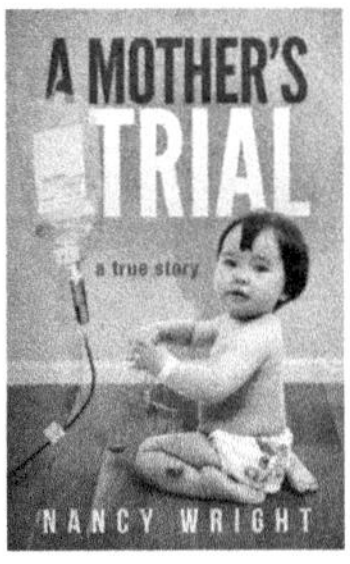

A Mother's Trial, by Nancy Wright
Info/buy:

Was it the perfect murder? A true story.

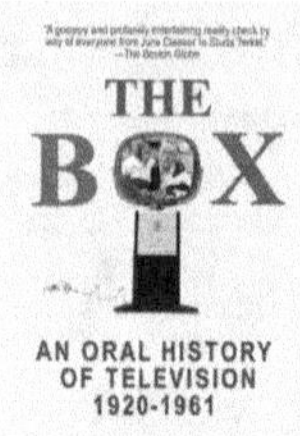

The Box: An Oral History of Television, 1920-1961, by Jeff Kisseloff

Info/buy:

"Wondrous... An oral scrapbook of the pioneering days of our video nation"—The New York Times Book Review

You Must Remember This: An Oral History of Manhattan from the 1890s to World War II, by Jeff Kisseloff

Info/buy:

Amazing stories of Manhattan from those who lived them.

Side Effects, by Harvey Jacobs

Info/buy:

Vonnegut meets Catch-22! In the last hours of his hectic life, Simon Apple faces up to the hard truth that his very survival represents a prescription for disaster, not only for the pharmaceutical industry but for the nation itself! From award-winning author Harvey Jacobs.

Local Knowledge (A Kieran Lenahan Mystery), by Conor Daly

Info/buy:

Lawyer-turned-golf pro Kieran Lenahan must solve the murder of millionaire country-club owner Sylvester Miles. "A FAST-PACED MYSTERY"—THE NEW YORK TIMES

The Sigil Trilogy (Omnibus vol.1-3), by Henry Gee

Info/buy:

The amazing Sigil Trilogy complete in one volume!